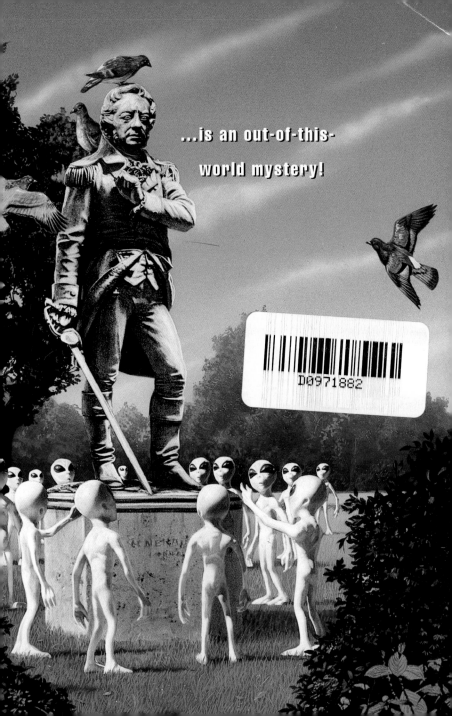

...is an out-of-this-world mystery!

D0971882

#3 THE EERIE TRIANGLE

2 WEIRD
EERIE
INDIANA

#3 THE EERIE TRIANGLE

MIKE FORD

AN AVON CAMELOT BOOK

This is a work of fiction. Names, characters, places and incidents either are the product of the author's imagination or are used fictitiously. Any resemblance to actual events, locales, organizations, or persons, living or dead, is entirely coincidental and beyond the intent of either the author or the publisher.

AVON BOOKS
A division of
The Hearst Corporation
1350 Avenue of the Americas
New York, New York 10019

Copyright © 1997 by Hearst Entertainment, Inc.
Based on the Hearst Entertainment television series entitled "Eerie Indiana"
Excerpt from *Eerie Indiana #4: Simon and Marshall's Excellent Adventure* copyright © 1997 by Hearst Entertainment, Inc.
Published by arrangement with Hearst Entertainment, Inc.
Visit our website at **http://AvonBooks.com**
Library of Congress Catalog Card Number: 97-93770
ISBN: 0-380-79776-3
RL: 4.5

First Avon Camelot Printing: October 1997

CAMELOT TRADEMARK REG. U.S. PAT. OFF. AND IN OTHER COUNTRIES, MARCA REGISTRADA, HECHO EN U.S.A.

Printed in the U.S.A.

OPM   10   9   8   7   6   5   4   3   2   1

PROLOGUE

*M*y name is Marshall Teller. Not too long ago, I was living in New Jersey, just across the river from New York City. It was crowded, polluted, and full of crime. I loved it. But my parents wanted a better life for my sister and me. So we moved to a place so wholesome, so squeaky clean, so ordinary that you could only find it on TV: Eerie, Indiana.

It's the American Dream come true, right? Wrong. Sure, my new hometown *looks* normal enough. But look again. Underneath, it's crawling with strange stuff. Item: Elvis lives on my paper route. Item: Bigfoot eats out of my trash. Item: I see unexplained flashing lights in the sky at least once a week. No one believes me, but Eerie is the center of weirdness for the entire planet.

No one except my friend Simon Holmes. Simon's my next-door neighbor. He's lived in Eerie his whole life, and he's the only other person who knows just how freaky this place is. Together we've been keeping a

1

record of all the stuff that happens around here. We've faced some of Eerie's most bizarre inhabitants and lived to tell about it, from the talking dogs that tried to take over the city to the crazy woman who kidnapped us and tried to keep us locked up forever in giant plastic kitchenware. I told you this place was weird.

Still don't believe me? You will.

1

*H*ow much do you know about your town's history? You know: how it was founded, who settled there, why it is the way it is, that kind of stuff. If you're like most people, you probably don't really know a whole lot about where you live. Maybe you see your town as just another boring collection of buildings.

But if you think about it, towns and cities are a lot like people. Each one has its own unique personality. Some are big and noisy—always on the go. Others are small and quiet and keep to themselves. The harder you look, the more you start to notice the little things that make your town different from all the other ones.

Then there's Eerie. As some of us know all too well, Eerie, Indiana, isn't like any other town in the entire United States. In fact, it's probably not like any other town in the whole world. No place is stranger, and no other place has as many bizarre inhabitants. But how does a town get to be so weird? I mean, something has to happen to a place to make it become a magnet for every freaky thing out there, right? It doesn't just happen for no reason.

Well, that's the question Simon and I set out to answer a couple of weeks ago. And what we found out was weirder—and got us into more trouble—than anything else we'd encountered before.

It all started with the statue of Zebediah Eerie. Actually it all started a little before that, in Miss Earhart's history class. If you want to know the truth, I actually *like* history class. I think it's cool to learn about what happened years ago, before I was even alive, when all of these people were running around discovering things no one had ever seen before and inventing new stuff that had never been invented.

It makes me imagine a bunch of kids sitting in a classroom a hundred years from now, maybe even reading about the things I did and saw while I was alive. Now that would be far out.

Anyway, we were talking about exploring. Miss Earhart had just finished telling us about how she'd spent the summer getting her pilot's license and taking some wild rides in her plane, and she was talking about the ancient city of Atlantis. Atlantis is this city that some people believe sank right into the ocean thousands of years ago. No one really knows where it might have been, so no one has ever found the ruins. But all kinds of weird things were supposed to have happened there, which is why people are so interested in it. That's what we were talking about.

"Atlantis was reported to be the center of many strange events," said Miss Earhart. "According to the little information we have about the city, all kinds of phenomena reportedly occurred there. One report talks about people changing into werewolves and mermaids. Another one claims that the Atlanteans could fly without machines."

I raised my hand. "Who were the Atlanteans?" I asked. "Where did they come from?"

"We don't really know," answered Miss Earhart. "Some people believe that Atlantis was created by aliens. In fact, it has even been suggested that the entire city was really a gigantic spaceship, and that it didn't sink into the ocean but flew up into the stars, taking everyone with it. But that's just a story, of course. We all know that aliens don't exist."

I could have told her a few things about aliens that might have made her change her mind about their existence, but I kept quiet about that. "Is there *any* proof that Atlantis ever existed?" I asked instead.

Miss Earhart shook her head. "Not really, Marshall," she said. "All we have to go on are some old manuscripts that mention the city. But none of them included maps, so we don't have a geographical location for it."

"So where do you think it is?" I asked.

"Well, I'm only an amateur explorer, so I can't really say. But I will tell you that I'm planning an expedition into the Bermuda Triangle over spring break to take a look around and see what's there."

The Bermuda Triangle. I'd read a lot about that in a book I'd found over the summer. The Bermuda Triangle is this really creepy part of the world where all sorts of weird stuff has happened. It's actually a giant area of the open sea. If you can imagine a big triangle drawn over the Atlantic Ocean with its three points resting on the tip of Florida and on the islands of Puerto Rico and Bermuda, that's the Bermuda Triangle.

According to the book I'd read, a lot of ships and planes have disappeared without a trace while sailing or flying through the Bermuda Triangle. They just up and vanished into thin air, sometimes even while people were watching from other planes or ships. A lot of pilots who fly through there say that their navigational instruments all go crazy or stop working when the plane is in the Triangle. Some boat captains have reported that their ships are surrounded by very heavy fog for hours at a time, and that their ships' clocks actually run backwards as long as they're in the Triangle.

The creepiest story I read was about a boat that sailed into the Triangle and was swallowed up by thick clouds. When it finally broke out of the clouds, it was a clear, sunny afternoon. Only it was thirty years and a day after the boat had first entered the Triangle. Everyone on it was the same age as before, though, and none of them could explain where they'd been.

"Do you think Atlantis might be in the Bermuda Triangle?" I said. If it was, that might explain all of the strangeness that went on there.

Miss Earhart smiled. "I can't say for sure," she said. "But I do think they might possibly be connected."

Before she could continue telling us more about Atlantis, the bell rang for the end of the day. I gathered up my books and left, but I didn't stop thinking about Atlantis and the people who lived there. It was hard for me to believe that such a bizarre place had existed and that no one had written more about it. No one knew exactly where it was. How could something like that happen?

I was still imagining what Atlantis must have been like as I got my jacket from my locker and headed outside. When I pushed open the front door of the school, I saw Simon waiting for me on the steps.

"Hey," I said. "How was your day?"

Simon sighed. "Don't even ask," he said. "I'm never going to make it through algebra. And in gym, Mr. Ripley made us hang from the chin-up bar to see if we could grow any taller. He said the first kid whose feet reached the floor would get a part in some show he's doing. Man, is he weird."

"I remember that," I said. "Wait until he puts you in the locked trunk and sees how long it takes you to get out."

"I can't wait. So how was your day? Any weirdness?"

"Not yet," I said. "But I've been thinking about something. What do you know about Eerie?"

"You mean besides the fact that it's the strangest place in the whole world?" said Simon.

"I know it's strange," I said. "But have you ever wondered *why* it's so strange? I mean, has it always been so weird, or is this something new?"

Simon thought for a minute. "I don't know," he said finally. "You're the only other person I've met who notices how strange it is. And now that you mention it, I don't really know anything about Eerie's history at all. I've never even heard anybody talk much about it."

While we talked, we were moving along the main street of town. We were just coming to the town hall, a brick building that sat on a lawn of green grass. I'd been inside the place a couple of times, but I'd never noticed much about it except for the statue that stood on a pedestal in front of the building.

It was a statue of a man. He was dressed in uniform, like a soldier, and his face looked stern. When I looked more closely I could see that his military boots were a bit shinier than the rest of the statue.

I stopped in front of it. "For instance," I said to

Simon. "Who's this guy? I've passed by this statue hundreds of times, but I have no idea who he is or why he's even here. What does he have to do with Eerie?"

Simon pointed to the base of the statue. "Why not just read the plaque?" he suggested. Good old Simon, always pointing out the obvious.

I knelt down and looked at the brass plate affixed near the statue's shiny boots. It was old, and it hadn't been cleaned in a long time. I had to rub a lot of dirt away before I could read the engraving.

"Zebediah Eerie," I read. "Founder of our beloved town."

That was it. There was nothing that said who exactly Zebediah Eerie was or what he'd done to get a whole town named after him.

"I didn't even know there was a real person named Eerie," Simon said.

"I didn't either," I said, standing up. "This is the first I've heard of him."

I looked at the statue of Zebediah Eerie again. "Don't you think it's weird that they never mention this guy in any of our classes?" I asked Simon. "We don't even have a founder's day picnic or anything. Back in New Jersey we always celebrated the date our town was founded. I had to write a paper on it, and every year there was a parade and the school marching band played our town song."

"I guess I just assumed Eerie has always been here," said Simon.

"Maybe it's time we did a little investigating," I said. "I want to know more about this Zebediah Eerie and who he was."

"What good will it do to get the scoop on some old dead guy?" asked Simon. "It sounds like a homework assignment to me, and I have enough of that to do."

"It isn't just about Zebediah Eerie," I explained. "It's about this whole town. I think if we find out more about Zebediah, we'll find out more about what's been happening here and why Eerie is so weird. It's just a hunch I have."

Simon groaned. "Okay," he said. "I'll do it. I know you won't give up anyway, so we might as well get it over with. What do we do?"

"It's really easy," I said, putting my arm around Simon's shoulder and walking up the steps toward the doors of the town hall. "All we have to do is go inside and get some information. Someone who works in there must know something about Mr. Zebediah Eerie. We're just going to ask a couple of questions. Trust me—nothing can go wrong."

"I've heard that one before," said Simon glumly as I pushed the door open and we went inside.

2

With Simon following reluctantly along behind me, I walked down the main corridor of the town hall, looking for someone who could help us.

"There's got to be an information office in here somewhere," I said.

No sooner had I spoken the words when we turned a corner and came to a door marked EERIE INFORMATION.

"See?" I said to Simon. "Look how easy that was. We'll be in and out of here in no time."

I turned the door knob and pushed the door open. The room we walked into was small but neatly arranged. The walls were covered with framed photographs that looked like they'd been taken a long time ago. There were file cabinets along one wall, and directly across from the door was a big desk. Behind it sat a young woman. Her hair was done up in a bun on top of her head, and she wore thick glasses. She was busily going through a book and crossing things out with a thick black marker. When she heard us come in, she looked up.

"Can I help you?" she asked. She seemed surprised to see us, as though no one had ever come in before.

"I hope so," I said, walking over to the desk. "My name is Marshall, and this is my friend Simon."

"How nice for you," the woman said. "I'm Miss Information."

"I guess you have the right job then, don't you?" I joked. "I mean, considering your name and all."

She smiled, but not in a friendly way. "I suppose I do," she said. "Now, what can I do for you boys?"

"Well," I said. "We need some information about Zebediah Eerie and how the town was founded."

Miss Information looked at me for a moment. "Really?" she said, raising one eyebrow. "May I ask why?"

I hadn't expected her to question me, and I wasn't sure what to say. From the tone of her voice, it sounded as though I'd asked for classified information that she wasn't supposed to give me without clearance. I tried to think of some excuse for why I wanted it that would sound reasonable, but my mind was blank.

"We need it for school," said Simon suddenly.

"Um, yeah," I said, taking his cue. "I have to do a project for my history class. You know, getting to know

12

all about your town. That kind of thing.'' I smiled, trying to look sincere.

Miss Information looked from me to Simon, then back again. Behind her glasses, her eyes seemed unnaturally big as she scanned our faces. Finally she put the cap back on her marker and laid it on the desk.

"I think I have just what you need," she said. She stood up and walked over to one of the filing cabinets. Opening the top drawer, she flipped through the files and pulled something out. Then she walked back to the desk and sat down again.

"Here you go,'' she said, pushing something toward me. It was a small booklet. Across the cover, printed in red ink, it said, *The History of Eerie: The Official Version.*

I picked up the booklet and flipped through it. It wasn't very long, and there were no pictures or anything.

"This isn't very extensive," I said. "Does it really have all the information about Eerie? You know, for my report.''

Miss Information nodded brusquely. "It contains everything you need to know," she said simply. "Is there anything else I can help you with?''

I put the booklet in my backpack. "I guess not," I said. "Thanks for the book.''

"You're very welcome," Miss Information said cheerfully. "Now have a very Eerie day."

She uncapped her marker and went back to reading the book. There was so much crossed out I didn't know how she could find anything left to look at, but she seemed to be enjoying herself. I turned around and left her there.

"That wasn't so bad," said Simon as we walked back down the corridor. "I mean, she was a little strange, but that's normal for Eerie."

"Let's go to my house and see what this brochure has to say," I said. "You can stay for dinner. I think we're having chicken."

"With potatoes?" asked Simon.

"Stuffing," I said.

"You're on!" crowed Simon.

We walked the rest of the way to my house and went up to the Secret Spot, which isn't really much of a secret since it's just my attic. But we do keep a lot of secret things up there in our Evidence Locker, like all the proof of Eerie's strangeness we've collected, and my journal. Simon stays over a lot, and we spend most of our time up there talking about what a weird town we live in.

"Okay," I said, flopping down on a chair. "Let's see what's in here."

I opened my backpack and took out the booklet Miss

Information had given me. I turned to the first page and started to read.

"The town of Eerie was founded in eighteen twelve by Zebediah Eerie. A jack-of-all-trades who came west from Virginia to seek his fortune, Zebediah spent several years attempting to locate gold in the hills of Montana. When this failed, he tried his hand at being a cowhand, but gave up when he was injured in a stampede after attempting to brand a bull.

"For a time, Zebediah wandered the country looking for work and performing odd jobs. Eventually he enlisted as a soldier, and fought with General William Henry Harrison in the Indian Wars. It was at the famous battle of Tippecanoe, in eighteen eleven, that Zebediah came face-to-face with his destiny and achieved his greatest success. On the morning of the battle, General Harrison awoke to find his favorite pair of leather boots missing. Shoeless, he feared he would not be able to lead his troops into battle. Zebediah, being of the same shoe size, volunteered to give the General his own boots, allowing the battle to go on and victory to be achieved.

"Because of Zebediah's bravery in the face of danger, Harrison gave him as a reward his choice of land in the reclaimed region. He chose a site which he felt was blessed with good luck and settled down there, building a cabin out of trees he cut down himself and planting a small vegetable garden. Believing that his boots had brought him luck, he took extra special care, shining and polishing his shoes for the rest of his life.

"Over time, other settlers came to Zebediah's land and asked to build homes there as well. Being a kindly man, he agreed. Shortly, a thriving town grew up around Zebediah's cabin. When Indiana was admitted to the Union in eighteen sixteen, the town officially became known as Eerie, Indiana."

"Wow," said Simon when I finished reading. "That's quite a story. I had no idea our founder was a hero. Is there anything else?"

"There's a little bit more," I said, flipping through the book. "But not much. Mostly stuff about how great it is to live here and how, statistically speaking, Eerie is the most normal place in the United States."

"Well, now we know why the statue's shoes are so shiny. Are you satisfied?" asked Simon. "Can I go back to just worrying about math now?"

"Not yet," I said. "According to this report, nothing even remotely interesting has happened here since Zebediah finished his cabin and settled down. But we know that isn't true. Something had to have happened here for things to get so mixed up. All Zebediah Eerie did was give some general his shoes and help win a battle. That doesn't explain anything. There has to be more to the story."

"But if that's all the book says, then that's all there is to know," said Simon. "You wanted to find out who Zebediah Eerie was, and now you have. Leave it alone, Mars."

"But don't you want to know what happened here?" I asked.

"No," said Simon. "I don't want to know. Really, I don't. It's bad enough living here and dealing with the weirdness. I'd rather not know any more about it than I have to."

I got off the chair and walked over to my desk. My parents had gotten me a new computer for my birthday. Simon and I were already using it to catalog all of the information we'd found out about Eerie. I also used it to write all of my school papers, and to keep track of which customers on my paper route had paid and which hadn't.

Best of all, I could use the computer to look up all kinds of cool stuff by connecting to other computers all over the place through the telephone line.

I turned on the computer and waited for it to start up. Simon pulled up a chair next to mine and watched while I opened up a file and clicked on it. The computer began to hum and buzz as it went to work.

"I'm signing on," I said. "This way we can search for some more information on Zebediah Eerie. If he was such an important figure, there must be something about him out there somewhere.''

The computer finished its start-up program and a box appeared asking me to type in some words describing what I was looking for.

"Let's try looking up the battle of Tippecanoe," I said, typing it into the computer.

The computer whirred and chirped to itself as it searched all the available files for information about Tippecanoe. After a minute, a list of places that had material about the battle appeared on the screen. There were quite a few. I selected the first one and clicked on it. A moment later, an article appeared.

Simon and I scanned the article, looking for any mention of Zebediah Eerie. The article talked about General William Henry Harrison. It gave figures for how many soldiers on each side were killed. It had information about the kinds of guns and swords that were used, and what battle strategies the different armies tried. But there was no mention of Zebediah Eerie giving General Harrison his boots. In fact, there was no mention of him at all.

"That's strange," said Simon when we'd finished reading the whole thing. "If Zebediah Eerie helped win the battle, you'd think they'd at least mention him *somewhere*."

We looked at four more articles that the computer

18

found, but they were all the same. Not one of them contained anything at all about the beloved shiny-shoed founder of our statistically normal town.

"Let's try looking him up by name," suggested Simon. "Maybe we'll find some articles that are just about him."

I typed Zebediah's name into the computer and hit the "enter" key. The computer buzzed and hummed for a long time, as though it was searching everywhere. Then a message appeared on the screen: NOTHING WAS FOUND MATCHING THAT ENTRY. PLEASE TRY AGAIN.

"It didn't find anything at all," I said. "Nothing. It's like he never existed."

I turned off the computer and leaned back in my desk chair. Something just wasn't right. If I had only been slightly interested in him before this, now I was fascinated.

"We need to find Zebediah," I said.

"Good idea, but how do you find a dead person?" asked Simon. "It's not like you can look him up in the phone book and give him a call."

"I have an idea," I said.

"I was afraid you'd say that," said Simon. "And just what might that idea be?"

I got up and grabbed my jacket. "Come on," I said. "We're going to the cemetery."

3

Simon and I put on our coats and went outside to the garage. Simon's bike was still at our house from the last time he'd spent the night. By taking the back roads, we got there in under fifteen minutes, and before long we were walking among the tombstones.

"Where do we look?" asked Simon.

I glanced around the cemetery. Most of the graves looked pretty much alike, so it was hard to tell if one area was older than the rest.

"Let's try over there," I said, pointing to a part of the cemetery where some of the tombstones had toppled over. "Maybe those fell over because they've been here longer."

We wound our way through the maze of graves, being careful not to step on any of the flowers that had been left there.

"I feel really creepy walking all over these dead people," said Simon. "Everywhere I go I'm afraid I'm stepping on them."

"Don't worry," I said. "If they don't like it, I'm sure they'll let you know."

"That's not funny," said Simon. "Remember what happened—"

The end of his sentence was cut off as he tripped over the edge of a stone and fell forward. He tumbled into the grass, and almost fell right into an open grave. He sat up, wiping the freshly dug dirt that covered his hands onto his pants.

"That was close," he said. "Another inch or two and I would have gone right into that thing."

"Don't worry," said a voice from inside the pit. "I would have helped you out."

All of a sudden, a dirt-covered face appeared right beside Simon. A big white grin broke out in the middle of the grime.

"Aaahhh!" Simon yelled, scrambling to get away from the face.

The head began to laugh. "Hang on, there," it said. "I'm not going to hurt you."

Simon had backed up against a gravestone. His face had turned white. I hate to admit it, but I was hiding *behind* the gravestone, peering out from around the side to see what was happening.

Two dirty hands appeared on the edge of the grave and a man lifted himself up onto the grass. Taking a handkerchief from his back pocket, he wiped some of the dirt away from his face. Then he put the handkerchief away and held out his hand to Simon.

"I'm Digger," he said. "The caretaker here."

Simon took Digger's hand and shook it. "Hi," he said. "I'm Simon." He looked around and saw me hiding behind the gravestone. "And that back there is my friend Marshall. This was all his idea."

"You two look like you've seen a ghost," said Digger. "I didn't mean to scare you. I was just trying to get this hole dug before night comes. I don't much like to be out here after dark. What are you two doing out here, anyway?"

"We're looking for someone," I said.

"Here?" said Digger. "Well, whoever it is, he can't have gone too far now, could he? Must be around here somewhere." He started laughing to himself at his joke.

"It's a dead someone," Simon said.

"Got plenty of those," said Digger. "Take your pick."

"We're looking for Zebediah Eerie," I said.

Digger stopped laughing. "Zebediah Eerie?" he said. "What do you want with him?"

"So you've heard of him?" I said excitedly. "He really exists?"

"Of course he exists," said Digger. "Or used to, anyway. Now he's just dead."

"Can you show us his grave?" I asked.

22

Digger looked around the graveyard. He seemed nervous. He wiped his hand across his forehead.

"I don't know," he said. "I'm not really supposed to take people in there." Digger pointed across the cemetery to a small building that sat on a little hill.

"What is it?" asked Simon.

"The crypt," said Digger. "It's where his tomb is."

"Why aren't you supposed to take anyone in there?" I asked him.

Digger looked around again. "It's—um—not really open to the public," he said. "Because it's so old. They don't want anyone getting hurt or anything."

"Who's 'they?' " I said.

Digger put his hands in his pockets. "The ones in charge," he said. He seemed really nervous now, like he was telling us something he wasn't supposed to and was afraid of getting in trouble.

"We won't touch anything," I said. "We just want to see Zebediah's tomb."

"Yeah," said Simon. "We have to do a report on it for school."

Digger looked at us. "For school, eh?" he said. "Guess that's okay, then. They can't get mad about me helping out some kids with their schoolwork, I guess."

He started to walk toward the crypt, and we followed him. It was getting dark now, and the cemetery was getting spookier by the minute. I was glad we were with Digger, but even so, I was anxious to get out of there.

"What do you know about Zebediah Eerie?" I asked as we walked.

Digger shrugged his shoulders. "Not much," he said. "He founded the town. Fought in some war or other. That's about it."

We came to the door of the crypt, and Digger took a ring of keys out of his pocket. He flipped through them for a minute looking for the right one, then stuck it into the lock. It turned with a grating sound, and he pushed heavily against the door. It creaked and groaned, but finally it swung open.

"Haven't been in here for a long time," he said as he went inside.

It was pitch black inside the crypt, and the air was colder than it was outside. The place smelled as though it hadn't been opened in a hundred years.

"It sure is dark," I said.

Digger took a flashlight out of his back pocket and turned it on. A thin beam of light shone around the crypt as he moved the light over the walls to show us what was in there.

"Not really much to see," he said. "Just the tomb, really."

He was right. The walls of the crypt were bare stone covered here and there with patches of green. The floor was also bare stone. But in the center of the room was a raised platform with a stone box on top.

"That's Zebediah?" I asked.

"That's him," said Digger. "Or what's left of him, anyway."

Simon and I walked over to the tomb. Like the rest of the crypt, it was plain old stone. There wasn't even any decoration on it or anything—just Zebediah's name carved into one end of the top.

"How come it doesn't say when he was born or when he died?" I asked Digger.

"No one knows," he said. "There was no record of his birth, and his death certificate can't be found."

"Shouldn't it have been in the town hall?" I said. "That's where they keep stuff like that, isn't it?"

"Usually," said Digger. "But there was a big fire a long time ago, and all of that stuff was burned up."

I leaned against the tomb. "I can't believe this man was the founder of our town and nobody knows anything about him at all," I said.

"Oh, someone knows," said Digger. "I had a lady come through here earlier this year. She knew all about old Zebediah. Came one afternoon and asked if she could see the tomb. She seemed nice enough, so I brought her in. In fact, that's probably the last time I was even in here."

"Who was she?" I asked. "Did she say how she knew about him? What did she want?"

"Slow down there," said Digger. "Let me think."

He rubbed his head for a minute, like that would help him to remember. Then he snapped his fingers.

"I remember now," he said. "She said she was doing some research for a newspaper article or something like that. Wanted to find out all about Eerie. Told her I'd only been working here about thirty years, so I didn't know a whole lot. Told her she should ask down at the information office in town."

"But who was she?" I asked.

Digger rubbed his head some more. He was rubbing it so hard I was sure a genie would pop out and grant me three wishes.

"Almost got it," he said, rubbing a spot right between his eyes. "Just a little more."

He polished his forehead in quick circles, then stopped. "I remember now!" he said. "Her name was Priscilla. Priscilla Bartlett. And she wasn't writing an article, it was a book. That's right. She was writing a book. Couldn't figure out why anyone would want to write a book about Eerie, but there you are. Some folks are just a little strange, if you know what I mean."

"Do you know what she found out?" I asked. I couldn't believe that someone else had been trying to get information about Zebediah and Eerie.

Digger shook his head. "Nope," he said. "Never saw her again. She just came that once. Told me she was interested in old Zeb here, just like you boys did. I gave her the grand tour and that was that."

"Did she say what she was looking for?" asked Simon.

"Just said she was writing a book," said Digger. "I can't remember any more than that. Like I said, I sent her on down to the information office. I never saw her again after that."

"I wish we knew what she was writing," I said. "Maybe she found something good."

Digger looked outside. The sun had almost completely set, and darkness was coming on fast.

"Well, we'd best be getting out of here," Digger said. "You boys seen enough?"

"I guess so," I said, taking one last look around. "Thanks for letting us in, Digger."

"My pleasure," he said. "Don't get too many visitors in here. It's nice to see some live faces every now and again." He chuckled to himself, and Simon and I joined in nervously.

The three of us left the crypt, and Digger locked it up again. Then he led us to the cemetery gates, where we had left our bikes. We hopped on and rode out, and Digger locked the gates behind us. He waved as we drove away, his flashlight swinging back and forth in the evening light.

Back at my house, Simon and I washed the dirt off of our hands and faces just in time for dinner. When we came downstairs, my father was just putting the chicken on the table. My sister, Syndi, and my mother were already sitting down.

"Look who's here," said my mother. "How was school, you two?"

"Normal," I said, picking up a piece of chicken and taking a bite.

"Well, why wouldn't it be?" said my father. "After all, this is Eerie, the most normal place on Earth."

I looked at Simon and rolled my eyes. Sometimes my parents are completely clueless.

"Hey, Dad," I said, waving a drumstick. "Did you ever hear of a woman named Priscilla Bartlett?"

He paused. "I don't think so, Mars, why?"

"Just wondering," I said. "Someone mentioned her today. Said she was writing a book about something I'm interested in. I thought maybe you might know who she was."

"Bartlett?" said Syndi, putting down her drumstick. "Did you say Priscilla Bartlett?"

"Yeah," I said. "You know her?"

"I remember something about her from my scrap-book," Syndi said.

My sister is totally normal in almost every way, from her normal haircut right down to her normal sneakers, but she has this one hobby that's pretty weird. She keeps this scrapbook that she fills with articles she finds about missing people. She's had it since she was about ten, when she saw this article in the newspaper about a man who vanished while he was camping in the woods near our old house. She cut it out and put it in this scrapbook my mom had bought her for putting pictures of her friends in. Ever since then, she's been cutting out these articles and saving them.

"What do you remember?" I asked.

Syndi took a bite of chicken. "She wrote a book," she said. "Something about UFOs or one of those nutsy things you're so into."

"So what happened to her?"

"That's just it," said Syndi. "Nobody knows. She was supposed to be researching her next book, but she wouldn't tell anyone what it was about. She said it was a secret. She went off one day saying she was doing research, but she never came back."

I looked at Simon. His eyes were wide.

"No one knows what she was writing about?" I asked. "Are you sure?"

"I'll show you the article after dinner if you want," said Syndi. "I only remember it because of the picture it had of her. She was really young and pretty, and I thought it was weird that she was into spacey stuff. She looked too normal.''

I looked at Simon again. He was staring at his chicken like he was afraid it would jump up and bite him. I knew he was thinking the same thing I was.

''Yeah,'' I said. ''Well, sometimes things aren't always what they seem.''

After dinner, Syndi got out her scrapbook and found the article about Priscilla Bartlett.

"I want that back when you're done," she said as she handed it to me. "And don't go getting your fingerprints all over it."

"Sure," I said, already reading the clipping as I walked away.

"What do you want to know about her for, anyway?" asked Syndi.

"School report," I said absentmindedly.

I took the article to the Secret Spot and closed the door. I sat down at my desk and read, while Simon looked over my shoulder and followed along.

AUTHOR MISSING, NO CLUES

Writer Priscilla Bartlett was reported missing on

Tuesday after failing to turn up at a lecture she was to give at the University of Pawtucket.

Bartlett is the author of the successful book *The UFO Conspiracy*, in which she charges that the government of the United States has been covering up evidence of alien visitations for years. She was scheduled to debate scientist Irving Coldwell, an expert in debunking UFO sightings, in what was expected to be a very well-attended event.

At the time of her disappearance, Bartlett was involved in researching her next book. While she refused to reveal the subject of her project to anyone, she said in a press release the day before her disappearance that she planned to present startling new evidence during the debate with Mr. Coldwell that would prove once and for all that the government had been involved in keeping the truth about extraterrestrials from the American public.

Police have no clues to Bartlett's disappearance. "It's like she vanished into thin air," said Detective Johnson Harper, who was called in to lead the investigation, which has so far turned up nothing.

"Who knows, maybe one of those aliens she wrote about came down and took her away, to keep her from telling their secrets."

Next to the article there was a picture of Priscilla Bartlett. Syndi was right, she was young. She was staring at the camera head-on, and you could tell she wasn't afraid of anything.

"I wonder what happened to her," said Simon.

"I don't know," I said. "But if Digger was telling the truth, then she was in Eerie right before she disappeared. And I bet the book she was working on was all about this town."

"What kind of proof do you think she had about UFOs? And what has that got to do with Eerie?"

I shook my head. "Whatever it was, someone didn't want her to tell anyone about it," I said.

Simon sat down on my bed. "I knew this was going to get us in trouble," he said. "I just knew it. I should never have agreed to go to the cemetery with you."

I put the article about Priscilla Bartlett into my notebook. "Too late," I said. "It looks like we've found ourselves another mystery. Tomorrow we'll look up her book in the library. Maybe that will give us some ideas about what to do next."

Simon sat up. "What?" he said sarcastically. "You mean we aren't going to go running around all night looking for clues or trying to dig up old Zebediah and see what he has to say about all this?''

"Very funny," I said. "I think we've done enough for today. Besides, I have some reading to do for tomorrow. Miss Earhart assigned us a whole chapter on the ancient Greeks.''

Simon took his coat from the hook on the door and put it on. "I'll see you tomorrow, then," he said. "I have some math to do, anyway.''

The next day, Simon and I didn't have a free period together until lunchtime. Instead of going to the cafeteria, we met at the school library. We went inside and headed straight for the card catalog, where we looked up Priscilla Bartlett's book.

Even though the B. F. Skinner Junior High School library isn't very big, it has an extensive collection of books about the supernatural and the unexplained, so I wasn't surprised to find out that they had two copies of *The UFO Conspiracy*. I went to the shelf where the card catalog said it was located. One of the copies was gone, but the other one was there. I took it to a quiet table in the back of the library and sat down.

"What are we looking for?" asked Simon as I opened the book and started flipping through the pages.

"Anything," I said. "I want to see what she has to say about aliens.''

The UFO Conspiracy was a collection of reports

about various UFO sightings and landings. According to Bartlett, each time someone reported seeing a UFO or found evidence of alien visitors, the government would make up a story saying that it wasn't true and trying to make everyone believe that there was a rational explanation for the events. She said that there was even a special government organization that did nothing but investigate alien encounters and then make them look like fakes.

A big part of the book was about something that happened in a town called Roswell, New Mexico. In 1947, people reported seeing lots of strange lights flashing in the night sky around Roswell. One night, several of the lights crashed to the ground and there was a huge explosion. Witnesses who rushed to the scene said that they saw what looked like two spaceships wrecked on the desert floor. But before they could get closer, soldiers appeared and ordered them out of the area. The soldiers then collected the spaceships and took them to a secret military base.

According to Priscilla Bartlett, those spaceships contained aliens. While some of them died, several survived the crash. The government sent scientists to study the aliens and to communicate with them as they recovered from their injuries. Everything that the scientists learned was written down and put into top-secret files. All the photographs of the aliens and their ships were also hidden away so that no one would ever see them.

Everyone involved with the Roswell incident was told to keep quiet about what they knew. The government issued an official report saying that the crashed ships were really weather satellites, and that there was no possibility of life in outer space at all. The whole area around Roswell was cleaned up so that no one could find any evidence of the aliens. Over the years, some of the soldiers and scientists involved in the capture and study of the aliens did tell their stories. But every time, the government denied any knowledge of anything weird happening in Roswell.

As for the aliens themselves, Bartlett said that they were hidden somewhere that only a few high-ranking government officials knew about. In a section called "Where Are They Now?" she wrote:

It is my belief that the aliens captured in Roswell were transported to a secret location, where they were held for further study. I believe also that there may be a connection between the Roswell aliens and unexplained phenomena reported throughout history, including the activity in the Bermuda Triangle, the construction of monuments at Stonehenge and Easter Island, and perhaps even the disappearance of the lost city of Atlantis.

"That's amazing," I said when I was finished reading. "If all this is true, then the government has known about aliens for a long time."

"But that still doesn't explain what Priscilla Bartlett was doing here in Eerie," said Simon. "What connection is there between the aliens and this place?"

"I'm not sure yet," I said. I was paging through the rest of the book, looking for anything else that might be interesting. In the center of the book there was a section of photographs, and I stopped to look at them. Most of them were pictures that people had taken of UFOs or strange lights in the sky.

One section of photos was taken at Roswell shortly after the soldiers arrived to investigate the explosions. They had been shot by a man who hid behind some rocks and wasn't spotted by the soldiers. They were sort of blurry because he'd been too excited to focus, but you could see some of the images pretty clearly. Most of the pictures showed soldiers running toward a pile of steaming metal that I guessed was the remains of a spaceship. Others showed bits of the spaceships being loaded onto trucks.

The most interesting pictures showed what were supposed to be the bodies of aliens being carried away on stretchers. Most of the aliens were covered up, but a few had their hands or feet hanging off the sides of the stretchers. They had long, thin fingers and toes that were sort of knobby on the ends. There were big bumps under the sheets where their heads would have been, which made me think that they would have had large heads and skinny bodies.

One figure appeared in most of the pictures. He was a tall man dressed in a black suit and wearing a black hat. He seemed to be in charge, because he was always pointing at something or telling someone something. The other people in the pictures seemed almost afraid of him. In the photos that showed the aliens on stretchers, he was walking alongside the stretchers, like he was making sure no one got near them.

"What a creepy-looking guy," said Simon.

"Isn't he?" I said. "I'd hate to run into him."

I shut the book and sighed. "Well, that was interesting," I said. "But I'm not sure how it fits together with Eerie. I think we should try to concentrate on finding out more about the history of this place. Let's go talk to Mrs. Ghostley."

Mrs. Ghostley was the school librarian. She was very small and very pale. In fact, sometimes she would appear right in front of you and you wouldn't even realize she was there until she said something. It was sort of spooky. She was always telling people to be quiet, but she seemed to know almost everything about everything, and she always knew just where to find whatever it was you were looking for.

Simon and I went over to her desk to look for her, but she wasn't there.

"Mrs. Ghostley?" I whispered as quietly as I could. "Are you here?"

"There's no need to shout," said a voice next to me, making me jump. I looked over, and Mrs. Ghostley was standing right beside me.

"Sorry," I said. "I didn't see you."

"What can I help you boys with?" she asked.

"We're interested in the history of Eerie" I said. "I was wondering if you had any books on it or anything."

Mrs. Ghostley laughed softly. I didn't know what was so funny, but she seemed to be amused. "Books on Eerie?" she said, as though it was the funniest thing she'd ever heard. "I don't think so. But I do have a special personal collection of my own. Would you like to see it?"

I looked at Simon. "Sure," I said.

Mrs. Ghostley walked into her office, motioning for us to follow her. She opened a cabinet and took out a big cardboard box, which she set on a table.

"I've been collecting these for a long time," she said, opening the box. "They're pictures of Eerie that I've found at garage sales and antique stores. Some of them are quite exciting."

"Are there any of Zebediah Eerie?" I asked.

"Oh, yes," said Mrs. Ghostley. "One very nice one. It was one of the few saved from the fire."

"The fire?" I said. "What fire?"

"Why, the fire that destroyed all of the records of Eerie," she said. "Everything was kept in the records department over at the town hall. But one night there was a fire, and it was all burned. Only a few things survived."

I remembered Digger saying something about a fire destroying all the information about Zebediah. "Can you show us the picture?" I asked.

Mrs. Ghostley took out a pile of old photographs and started to leaf through them. Halfway through the stack, she stopped and pulled one of the photos from the bunch.

"Here it is," she said, putting it on the table.

The photo showed a group of people standing in front of a cabin. The man in the center looked just like the statue of Zebediah Eerie. He was wearing the same uniform and shiny boots. He wasn't smiling.

"This was taken when the first group of settlers arrived in Eerie," said Mrs. Ghostley.

I looked at the rest of the people in the photo. The women were wearing old-fashioned dresses and bonnets. They looked dirty and tired, as though they'd had a very long journey. Some of them held babies in their arms.

The men were dressed in work pants, shirts, and boots. Most of them had big moustaches.

All except one. Off to one side there was a man who didn't seem to quite belong to the rest of the group. Instead of looking at the camera, he was looking at Zebediah Eerie. And instead of wearing work clothes, he was dressed in a black suit and hat.

For a few seconds, I just stared at the man, trying to figure out why he looked familiar. At first I thought it was just that he didn't quite fit in. But then it came to me. I'd seen him before. In fact, I'd seen him just a few minutes ago.

It was the same man from the pictures taken at the Roswell alien crash site, only the photo I was looking at now had been taken over one hundred years earlier.

5

I looked more closely at the photograph. There was no doubt about it—the man was the same one from the pictures in Priscilla Bartlett's book. He was even wearing the same suit.

"Where did you say you got this picture?" I asked Mrs. Ghostley.

"Why Mayor Chisel himself gave it to me," she said. "After the fire, he thought that the remaining pictures of old Eerie should be kept all together someplace safe. He gave me what was left over from the fire. Wasn't that kind of him?"

She laid out several more pictures on the desk. Some showed rows of cabins; others were of people plowing fields or hanging up clothes on lines strung between trees. Altogether, there were about twenty pictures.

"This is one of my favorites," she said, picking up a picture. "It's the first general store in Eerie."

I looked at the picture. A group of men were standing in front of a building. There was a big ribbon across the front door, and a sign over the porch said EERIE MERCANTILE in handwritten letters.

"Hey," said Simon. "That's World of Stuff!"

He was right. The building looked a lot different now, but it still had the same doors. I looked more closely at the men in front. One of them looked suspiciously familiar.

"That's Mr. Radford!" I exclaimed, pointing to a man smiling and waving at the camera.

"Not quite," said Mrs. Ghostley. "That's his great-great-great grandfather, Cornelius Radford."

"It looks exactly like him," I said. "They even have the same glasses."

"And look there," said Simon, pointing to the man about to cut the ribbon with a big pair of scissors. "He looks just like Mayor Chisel. I'd know that creepy smile anywhere."

"The Chisels have been mayors here for many years," said Mrs. Ghostley. "It runs in the family."

"You say that some of these pictures were given to you by the mayor?" I asked.

"Yes. They're quite a treasure. I'm so pleased he gave them to me. I guess he knew I'd make sure that they were taken care of."

"Well," I said. "Thank you for showing them to us."

Mrs. Ghostley smiled. "Oh, you're very welcome, dear. Any time you want to see them, you just ask."

Mrs. Ghostley started to put the pictures back into the box when I had an idea.

"Do you think we could maybe get copies of the pictures of Zebediah and the one of the Eerie Mercantile?" I asked.

Mrs. Ghostley frowned. "Well," she said. "I'm not really supposed to. I don't remember why exactly, but the mayor said it wouldn't be good to have too many copies of them floating around. But you're nice boys, so I don't see why not."

She took the two pictures to the photocopier behind the desk and made copies. Then she came back and handed them to me.

"These aren't the clearest copies," she said.

"Oh, they're just fine," I said. "Thank you."

Mrs. Ghostley put the photos back in the box and stored it once more in the cabinet, which she was very careful to lock. Then she walked us out of the room and went back to work at the front desk.

"Can you believe how much those guys look like Chisel and Radford?" said Simon when we were back at our table, looking at the copies of the pictures.

"If you ask me," I said. "They look a little *too* much like Chisel and Radford."

"What do you mean?" asked Simon.

I pointed to the picture of Zebediah Eerie and told him about recognizing the man from the Roswell photographs.

"Something isn't adding up," I said. "There's no way he could have been alive for more than a hundred and thirty-five years."

"But that's Zebediah Eerie in the picture," said Simon. "See, he looks just like the statue. He even has the same shiny boots."

"I know," I said. "It doesn't make sense."

I thought for a minute. Then I had an idea. "Come over here," I said to Simon, heading for the reference section. "I want to look something up."

I walked down the aisles between the shelves of reference materials until I came to the atlases. I took one down and opened it to the index.

"What are you looking for now?" asked Simon. "These are just a bunch of old maps."

"Exactly," I said. "I want to look at something."

I turned to the map of Indiana and ran my fingers over the various coordinates until I found what I wanted.

"See?" I said to Simon.

"What?" he said, staring at the page. "I don't see anything."

"That's the whole point," I said. "This is a map of Indiana in eighteen sixteen, right after it was admitted to the Union as the nineteenth state. According to the brochure we got from Miss Information, Eerie was already an official town then. But it's nowhere on this map."

I flipped to another page and another map. "This is the same map, but from eighteen fifty-nine," I said. "Look, there still isn't anything where Eerie should be."

Sure enough, there were a lot of little towns—like Fateful, Blessing, and Round Bottom—scattered around the area where Eerie was supposed to be. But there was still no Eerie.

"Maybe they just forgot to put it on there because it was so small," Simon said.

"Maybe," I said. "But that seems too coincidental. Let's keep looking."

We looked at four more maps of Indiana, from 1879, 1903, 1918, and 1939. While a lot of things about the state changed over those years, one thing remained the same: Eerie, Indiana, didn't appear on a single map. On each one, the land that Eerie sat on was listed as empty wilderness.

Finally we turned to the map from 1948. I found the coordinates and looked at that section of the page, fully expecting to find blank space just like before. But this time, Eerie was there. And where Lake Winnetonga and Mount Bolger had been, Lake Eerie and Mount Eerie were in their places.

"Hey," said Simon. "There we are!"

"It's about time," I said.

I studied the map, looking for any other details that might be there. In between the shaded parts indicating different land elevations, I noticed that there were some dotted lines going around Eerie that seemed to form a pattern.

"Do you have a pencil?" I asked Simon.

"I think so," he said, checking his back pocket. "Yeah, I do. Here."

I took the pencil and started to connect the dotted lines around Eerie.

"What are you doing?" Simon whispered. "You can't write in a library book."

"Ssshhh," I said. "This might be important. I can always erase it later."

I connected one series of dots. It started at Lake Eerie and went down toward the right side of the map at an angle. When I came to the end, at Mount Eerie, the dots started to go back up at an opposite angle, forming a V shape.

"What are those?" asked Simon as I drew the second line.

"I think they're town boundary lines," I said. "If I

47

connect them, it will show us how big Eerie is and what shape it is."

The second line ended exactly where the Eerie Woods were. From there, the dots went back to the left in a straight line, ending right back where I had originally started. I took the pencil away and looked at what I'd drawn.

"It's a triangle," said Simon.

It was. Eerie's borders formed a perfect triangle around the center of town, with Lake Eerie, Mount Eerie, and the Eerie Woods at the three corners.

"That's really weird," said Simon.

"No," I said. "It's Eerie. It's the Eerie Triangle."

"You mean just like the Bermuda Triangle?" said Simon incredulously.

"Exactly," I said.

Simon looked at me. "So what you're saying here is that Eerie never even existed until nineteen forty-seven. Not only that, but when it does finally appear, it's in the exact shape of the Bermuda Triangle, the weirdest place on the planet."

"The *former* weirdest place on the planet," I said. "And yes, that's what I'm saying."

"But what about those pictures that Mrs. Ghostley has?" said Simon. "Those were taken way before nineteen forty-seven."

"Maybe they were," I said. "And maybe they weren't."

"What do you mean?"

"I think we're going to go have a talk with Mr. Radford after school," I said.

Simon and I got our backpacks and left the library just as the bell was ringing. He went off to science class, and I headed for English. For the rest of the day, I tried to fit all the pieces of the Eerie puzzle together in my head, but there were still some holes. Some big holes.

When the last bell rang, I dashed to my locker and then out the doors. Simon was there already, and we walked quickly toward World of Stuff. I had a few questions I wanted to ask Mr. Radford.

When we got to the store, it was pretty much empty. A few kids were standing around reading the latest comic books, and there was an old woman rummaging through the Halloween decorations, but that was it. Simon and I took some seats at the soda fountain and waited for Mr. Radford to notice us. He was trying to get the cotton candy machine to work, and he'd gotten a big wad of blue spun sugar wrapped around his hand.

"Drat," he said. "This will make it very difficult to wear mittens this winter."

I cleared my throat, trying to get his attention. He was pulling gobs of cotton candy from between his fingers, and didn't hear me. I did it again, and he turned around.

"What?" he said. "Oh, hello, boys. How are you today?"

"Just fine, Mr. Radford," I said.

"So, what can I do for you? Malted milks? Butterscotch sundaes? What will it be?" He was still struggling with the sticky candy.

"Nothing like that," I said, taking the copies of the photographs out of my backpack and unfolding them. "We just have a few questions for you."

"Questions?" said Mr. Radford "Why? Am I under arrest?" He laughed at his own joke. "I'm innocent, I tell you. Innocent."

"Um, right," I said. "No, we just had some questions about your ancestor."

"My ancestor?" said Mr. Radford. His hand had gotten stuck to his pants, and he was trying to get unstuck.

I pushed the copy of the picture showing the grand opening of the Eerie Mercantile across the counter. "Maybe this will help," I said.

Mr. Radford tried to pick up the picture, but it got stuck to the cotton candy on his fingers. He held it up in front of his face.

"Why, look at that," he said. "That fellow looks just like me, doesn't he?"

"You mean you don't recognize him?" I said.

50

"Should I?" said Radford. He suddenly sounded a little uncertain.

"That's your great-great-great-grandfather, Cornelius Radford," I said, "at the grand opening of this store."

Mr. Radford looked harder at the picture. Then he grinned. "Of course. Of course. Grandfather Cornelius. Wonderful man. I remember the day that was taken. Lovely day. Very sunny."

"How could you remember it?" I said. "You weren't even born. It was over a hundred years ago."

"Oh, of course it was," said Mr. Radford. "You're right. You're right. I couldn't possibly have been there."

"But this *is* your great-great-great-grandfather, right?"

"Sure it is," said Mr. Radford, trying to get the picture off his hand by shaking it. "If you say so. Who else would it be? Now, is there anything else I can do for you? I'm very busy right now."

I pulled the picture off of Mr. Radford's hand and wiped away the remains of the cotton candy. Suddenly he seemed to want to get away from us. I held up the other picture—the one of the man in black. When he saw it, his eyes went wide and his face drained of color.

"What's the matter?" I said. "You look like you've seen a ghost."

"No," he said. "No ghost. Nothing like that."

"Do you recognize the man in the black suit?" I asked him. "We're trying to figure out who he is."

"Never seen him before," said Mr. Radford. "Couldn't tell you who he is."

"Are you sure?" I asked. "Look again."

Mr. Radford wouldn't look at the picture. "Like I said, I've never seen him. Would you boys like some sodas?"

I put the picture back in my backpack. "No, thanks," I said. "We have some homework to do. But thanks for the information."

"Anytime," said Radford. "Anytime."

As Simon and I left the store, I saw Mr. Radford pick up the phone behind the soda fountain and dial a number.

"Hello, Mayor," I heard him say as the door swung shut. "I think we have a little problem."

*B*ack at my house, in the safety of the Secret Spot,
Simon and I made plans for what to do next. I
knew we were onto something, and we had to be
careful.

"I know Radford was hiding something," I said.
"This picture made him really nervous, especially
seeing the man in the black suit. I think he knows a lot
more than he's telling us. Besides, I heard him calling
the mayor as we were leaving."

"What would Radford and the mayor have to hide?"
said Simon. "I mean *this* time."

"I don't know," I said. "But I think it's something
big, and I think it has to do with the fact that Eerie
doesn't appear on any maps until nineteen forty-eight,
and that when it finally does, it looks an awful lot like
the Bermuda Triangle."

"We need more information," I said. "And what

better place to get information than an information office.''

''We already tried that,'' said Simon. ''It didn't get us anywhere.''

I smiled. ''That's because we went about it the wrong way,'' I said. ''This time we're going to do it differently. We're going to go after hours.''

''You mean break in?'' exclaimed Simon.

''Exactly,'' I said. ''Just meet me in front of the statue of Zebediah at nine o'clock,'' I said. ''And make sure you wear dark clothes.''

After dinner I told my parents that I was going upstairs to study. Then I locked my bedroom door, turned on the radio to make it sound like I was working in there, and changed into black jeans and a black shirt. I picked up my backpack and opened my window. Simon and I had made a rope ladder that we used whenever we wanted to go exploring late at night and didn't want to use the front door. I tossed it out the window and then climbed out and down to the ground.

I made it to the town hall in under ten minutes and went straight to the statue of Zebediah Eerie. Simon wasn't there.

''Simon?'' I whispered. ''Simon? Are you here?''

''I'm right here,'' said a voice in the darkness.

I turned around. ''Where?'' I said. ''I don't see you.''

Simon stepped out of the shadows. He was dressed all in black, including a black cap. Even his face was painted black.

"What's all over your face?"

"Some makeup I had left over from Halloween," he said. "Is it dark enough?"

"It's a little much, " I said. "But it works. Now let's get going."

Checking to see that no one was walking by, we dashed up to the town hall and skirted around the side of the building until we were hidden from view.

"How will we get in?" asked Simon.

"Look for a window we can open," I said.

We walked to the back of the building. There were a lot of windows, but all of them were too high off the ground to reach. Then I noticed a small window near the ground.

"That one," I said. "That's our way in."

We went over to the window and looked inside. It was too dark to see, so I took a flashlight out of my backpack and shined it inside.

"It looks like the basement," I said.

There was no way to open the window, so I had to break it. Telling Simon to stand back, I kicked the glass and listened to the pieces tinkle onto the floor below. Then I carefully removed the jagged pieces left around the edges and stuck my head through.

"It's only a few feet to the floor," I said to Simon. "If we lower ourselves through, we can just drop down."

I went first. Lying on my stomach, I put my legs through and slid my body into the basement. Then I let go of the windowsill and dropped to the floor. I could feel bits of broken glass beneath my feet, but I was fine.

"It's okay," I said to Simon. "Come on down."

I watched as Simon's feet came through the window, followed by the rest of him. He let go, and I steadied him as he dropped into the basement.

"Well, we're not going to be able to get back up there," he said. "I hope this plan of yours includes another way out."

I switched on the flashlight again and shined it around. The basement was filled with boxes and other assorted odds and ends. A furnace hummed in the corner, and on one wall hung the giant candy canes that decorated the town hall every Christmas. The big black box that was used to hold the Eerie lottery every seven years sat nearby, covered in dust.

On the other side of the room from the window, a stairway went up.

"This way," I said, walking across the basement.

We went up the stairs and came to a door at the top. Thankfully, it wasn't locked. We pushed it open and found ourselves in the main hallway.

"Jackpot," I said. "This is right where we want to be."

We walked down the hall until we came to the information office. I turned the knob, expecting to find it locked. Much to my surprise, it swung open easily.

"We're in," I said to Simon, who gave me a thumbs-up sign.

We went into the office and closed the door. Then I switched on the light.

"Now we can really look around," I said.

"What are we looking for, exactly?" asked Simon.

"Anything unusual," I said. "Try the file cabinets first."

Simon went over to the file cabinets, while I went to Miss Information's desk.

"They're locked," Simon said, rattling the drawers uselessly.

"That doesn't matter," I said. "Come look at this."

Sitting on top of Miss Information's desk was the book she had been writing in with the black marker when we first saw her. I was flipping through the pages, looking at what she'd crossed out.

"What is it?" asked Simon, coming over to take a look.

I showed him the cover. It was Priscilla Bartlett's book, *The UFO Conspiracy*.

"This must be the second copy that's missing from

57

the library," I said. "Look, she's gone through and crossed out all sorts of information. It's almost like she's trying to make sure no one can read it."

I turned to the pages with the photos. Several of them had been cut out, including the one of the man in the black suit at Roswell.

"Why would Miss Information be interested in a book about UFOs?" said Simon.

"I don't know, but let's keep looking for stuff. I have a feeling what we're looking for is going to be in here."

I opened the top drawer of her desk. It looked like any other desk drawer, filled with pencils and paper clips and rubber bands. I glanced through the mess of index cards and rubber stamps, but there was nothing interesting.

I moved on to the file drawer on the side of her desk. It was crammed with file folders. They were all labeled with names like VISITOR INFORMATION, TOURIST QUESTION-NAIRES, and EMPLOYEE EVALUATIONS.

"There's nothing here," I said. "Just a lot of forms and stuff."

Before I could decide where to look next, I heard a clicking sound. It was coming from the hallway, and it sounded like footsteps coming toward the office.

"Someone's coming!" I said to Simon. "Quick, turn off the light and hide."

Simon hit the light switch, pitching the room into

blackness. Then he ran back to the desk, tripping over a chair and almost falling. He put his hand over his mouth so he wouldn't cry out from the pain in his foot.

"Under here," I said, pointing to the desk. Simon scrambled into the space where the desk chair would go, and I followed him. It was an extremely tight fit with both of us under there, and if anyone came behind the desk, they'd be sure to see us. My heart was beating wildly in my chest as I waited to see what would happen.

A second later, the door opened. Someone turned on the light.

"I can't believe you just left it out in the open," said a man's voice. "Especially with the door unlocked."

"I'm sorry," said a voice that I identified as Miss Information's. "But as soon as you told me that Radford called, I hurried out to make sure everything was safe."

Once she said that, I recognized the man's voice. It was Mayor Chisel. "We can't afford screwups like that," said the mayor.

"Well, everything looks fine," said Miss Information. "I'll just grab the book and we'll go."

She walked over to the desk, her high heels clicking on the floor. I looked at Simon. His eyes were wide with fear. I crossed my fingers. I could see her shadow coming closer and closer.

Miss Information stopped right in front of the desk. I heard her pick up the book.

"Got it," she said. "Now let's go."

"I hope you don't leave everything just lying around like that," said the mayor. "What if someone found the map?"

Miss Information laughed. "Don't worry," she said. "I put it where no one would ever think to look. It's in a file marked VACATION PLANS."

The mayor laughed. "Good thinking," he said.

There was a click as someone turned off the light switch. Then I heard the sound of a key in the door. I waited until the sounds of footsteps disappeared, then I came out from under the desk.

"That was too close," said Simon. "One more step, and she would have seen us."

"That was the mayor she was with," I said. "What are they doing together?"

"And what's this map they were talking about?" said Simon.

"I don't know," I said. "But let's see if we can find it."

I opened the file drawer again and started combing the various folders. I found the one labeled VACATION PLANS and pulled it out. Inside, hidden under a stack of employee vacation forms, there was a map.

"What's it a map of?" asked Simon.

I looked at it closely. "It looks like a map of Eerie," I said. "At least part of Eerie. See? Here's the town hall."

The map showed the town hall in the center. A long thick line ran from one part of the hall to another part of Eerie, where it ended in a big *X*.

"What is that?" said Simon. "A road or something?"

"It can't be," I said. "If it was a road, it would run right through houses and stores and stuff. This would have to run underground. And it ends right in the middle of the Eerie Cemetery."

"Why would there be a road from the town hall to the cemetery?"

"Maybe it isn't a road," I said. "Maybe it's a secret passage of some kind. That would explain why it's underground."

"But what's in the middle of the cemetery?" said Simon.

We looked at each other. "Zebediah Eerie's tomb!" we said at the same time.

"Something is in that crypt," I said. "Something they don't want anyone to know about. We have to get inside there."

"How are we going to get in there?" said Simon. "We can't even get out of here. She locked us in when she left, remember?"

I looked at the map again. "If this *is* an underground passage," I said, "the entrance has to be in here somewhere. See? It ends right at the edge of the building. We just have to figure out how to open it."

I looked around the office for anything unusual. Apart from the pictures lining one wall, there wasn't much of anything else. I certainly couldn't see anyplace where there might be a hidden opening to a secret passage.

I sat down in Miss Information's desk chair and looked around at the things on her desk. It all looked perfectly ordinary. There was a pencil holder, a note pad for telephone messages, and a telephone.

I looked at the telephone. It had a lot of buttons on it with different names written in next to them, so Miss Information could dial the numbers just by hitting the buttons. The top one had MAYOR written next to it, followed by VIDEO STORE, LIBRARY, DENTIST, WORLD OF STUFF, and MOM. The last button had ZEBEDIAH written in next to it.

"I have an idea," I said to Simon.

I picked up the phone. There was a dial tone. I hit the button that said ZEBEDIAH, and I heard a series of beeps, like a number was being dialed. But there was no ring on the other end. Instead, the row of filing cabinets against the wall slid back and disappeared.

"Wow!" said Simon. "How did you do that?"

"I just reached out and touched someone," I said.

I hung up the phone and went to look at the place where the filing cabinets had been. In their place was a set of steps going down into the ground. The tunnel was dark, and it smelled stale and wet.

I picked up my backpack and slung it over my shoulder.

"Let's go," I said, switching the flashlight on. "We have an appointment with a dead man."

7

We walked down the steps and into the black mouth of the tunnel. As I descended the stairs, using the flashlight to see what was in front of me, I felt the air grow colder with each step. I could tell we were pretty far underground because the stone walls of the tunnel were covered with thick patches of greenish moss, and everything felt damp.

"Someone went to a lot of trouble to build this," said Simon. "I wonder how they did it without anyone noticing."

"I have a feeling this tunnel was built exactly so that people wouldn't notice," I said. "Whoever built it wanted to hide something."

The tunnel stretched on in front of us for what seemed like miles. There were a few twists and turns, but other than that we just kept walking through the silent stone hallway. We'd been walking for almost half an hour, and I had no way of knowing just how far we'd gone, or when we might come to the end.

"What do you think we're going to find?" asked Simon.

"I don't know," I said. "But we have to be ready for anything."

I was starting to wish I'd never even started looking into the history of Eerie. Every new discovery was taking me one step further into a mystery I didn't know how to solve. But I couldn't tell Simon that, not after I'd dragged him into it. All I could do was keep walking.

Just as I was wondering if the tunnel would ever end, I saw something appear in the circle of brightness made by the flashlight. It was another set of stairs. Only this set led up and out of the darkness.

"Well," I said to Simon. "Whatever is waiting for us is right up those stairs. Are you ready?"

"Ready as I'll ever be," he said.

I approached the stairs and shined the flashlight up them. They seemed to vanish about twelve steps up.

"They must turn a corner," I said. "I can't see beyond that."

We walked up the stairs until we came to the turn. I carefully poked my head around the corner and looked to see what came next. It was more stairs, ending in an open doorway. We went up the remaining steps and stopped.

Beyond the doorway was a room. Like the tunnel, it was made of stone walls, only it was much larger than the tunnel. There were no windows or other doors. We stepped inside and saw that the room was filled with all sorts of strange stuff, like piles of old clothes and hats.

"What is all this?" I said, picking up an old-fashioned coat that was lying in a heap on the floor. "It looks like the costume room for a theater or something."

"I'll say it does," said Simon. "Look at this."

He picked up a jacket and put it on. It was a leather coat with fringe on the sleeves and pockets. Then he picked up a hat and placed it on his head. It was an old coonskin cap. I laughed at the sight of him. The coat was much too big, and the sleeves dangled below his hands. The hat almost covered his eyes.

"You look like Davy Crockett," I said.

Simon posed, putting his hand up to his head. "At your service, sir," he said.

I stopped laughing. Something about the way Simon was standing reminded me of something.

"Simon," I said. "Do you know what you have on?"

"Yeah," he said. "A silly costume."

I shook my head. "No," I said. "That's Zebediah's coat and hat."

"Get it off me!" Simon shrieked. "Get it off. I'm wearing a dead man's clothes."

He tore the jacket off and threw it on the floor, then snatched the cap from his head and held it in his hands, looking at it in horror. I picked up the jacket and examined it.

"This is his, all right," I said. "I recognize it from the pictures."

"Why is it down here?" said Simon.

I shined the flashlight on the piles of clothes and started to pick through them. After a minute of searching, I looked up.

"We were right about one thing," I said. "These *are* costumes. But they aren't from any play. They're from the photographs of Eerie."

"What do you mean?" said Simon.

I held up a shirt I'd found. "See this? This is the shirt the mayor was wearing in that picture. I recognize the funny collar. Only this shirt isn't that old. None of these clothes are."

I looked at the inside of the shirt. "Besides," I said, "where would someone from the eighteen hundreds get a shirt made in Taiwan?"

"So you're saying those pictures aren't real?"

I nodded. "They're real, but they weren't taken in the eighteen hundreds," I said. "They're fakes, made to make us think that Eerie has been around that long. That's why Radford and the Mayor look so much like the guys in the picture."

"Because they *are* the guys in the picture," said

Simon as he figured it out. "But why would they want to do that?"

"If we knew the answer to that," I said, "we wouldn't have to be here. Let's keep looking."

I looked around the room some more. The more closely I looked, the more I recognized props from the pictures I'd seen, including hoes, shoes, and even baby bonnets.

"Look at this," I said, shining the light into a corner. Leaning up against the wall was the sign from the Eerie Mercantile, the letters still as fresh as they were in the photograph.

I walked over and took hold of the sign. When I tried to pull it away from the wall, it started to rise up into the air.

"Stand back!" I said to Simon.

The sign slid up, almost to the ceiling. As it did, a doorway was slowly revealed. I watched as, inch by inch, the door opened. When it was almost all the way up, I shined the light inside the newly revealed room. It was much smaller than the main room, and it had a bed in it. Sitting on the bed, pressed up against the wall, was a person.

I shined the light on the figure huddled on the bed.

"Who is it?" said a quavering voice. "What do you want now? I've told you everything."

It was a woman. I went closer to the bed.

"It's okay," I said. "We won't hurt you. We're here to help."

The woman took her hands away from her face. What I saw almost made me drop the flashlight. It was Priscilla Bartlett.

Her skin was very pale, and her hair was longer, but it was her. She looked just like her picture in the newspaper article, except now she looked scared.

"You!" I said. "What are you doing here?" I turned to Simon. "It's her. Priscilla Bartlett."

I turned back to Priscilla. "We read your book," I said. "It was great."

She was still staring at me. "Who are you?" she said.

"I'm sorry," I said, feeling like an idiot. "I didn't mean to scare you. I'm Marshall, and this is Simon."

"How did you find me?" she asked. She was still really nervous. "Are you with them?"

"Them?" I said. "Them who? We found this map in Miss Information's office, and we followed it here."

"Miss Information!" shrieked Priscilla hysterically. "She didn't follow you, did she?"

"No," I said. "Why?"

Priscilla sat up straighter on the bed and fussed with her hair. "It's a long story," she said. "I guess I'd better start at the beginning."

Simon and I sat on the floor and listened to Priscilla as she told us what had happened to her.

"I was working on my second book," she said. "And I came to Eerie to do some research."

"Digger told us that," I said.

Priscilla nodded. "Yes, Digger was nice enough to let me see Zebediah's tomb. I don't think he's one of them. Or if he is, he doesn't know what they're doing."

"One of them who?" said Simon. "You keep saying that."

"I'll get to that," said Priscilla. "After I saw the tomb, I wanted to get some more information about Eerie, so I went to the information office."

"Just like we did," I said. "I bet Miss Information gave you the same brochure. The one about the history of Eerie."

"She did," said Priscilla. "Only I knew it was a lie, and I said so. That was my big mistake. I didn't realize at the time that she was part of the whole thing. I insisted on seeing the mayor."

"So the mayor *is* in on it," I said. "I knew it."

"I'd gotten hold of some pictures of Eerie," said Priscilla. "And I took them to the mayor's office."

"The ones of Zebediah and of the Eerie Mercantile?" I asked.

"That's right. I suspected they were fakes, so I wanted to confront the mayor face-to-face and see what he would say. I had no idea he would do what he did."

"What was that?" asked Simon.

"He kidnapped me," said Priscilla. "Well, not just him. They all did. There I was, sitting in his office asking him some questions. I really thought I had him where I wanted him. Then, all of a sudden, someone came up behind me and slipped a rag soaked in something over my mouth and nose. I passed out, and then the next thing I knew, I was in here."

"You've been here for almost five months?" I said.

"Has it been that long?" said Priscilla. "I stopped counting after the third month."

"But how do you survive?" I asked.

Priscilla sighed. "They feed me," she said. "And sometimes they bring me things to read. But nothing interesting."

"But who are they, and why are they keeping you?" I said. "What exactly is going on here?"

Priscilla took a deep breath. "Aliens," she said. "It's about aliens."

I looked at Simon. "What aliens?"

"You read my book, right?" said Priscilla. "Do you remember the part about Roswell, New Mexico?"

We both nodded.

"Well," said Priscilla, "the government has always denied that anything happened there, but I've never believed it. My theory was that they simply took the aliens who landed in Roswell and moved them somewhere else. Somewhere no one would ever think of looking."

"Like where?" I said, even though I thought I knew.

"If you were going to hide aliens," she said, "where would you want to put them?"

"The most normal place on earth?" I said.

She nodded. "Exactly."

"You mean the aliens are right here in Eerie?" said Simon.

"Not just that," said Priscilla. "I think that Eerie was invented just so they would have a place to hide them."

"It all makes sense now," I said. "Eerie didn't appear until nineteen forty-eight, the year after Roswell. Zebediah Eerie isn't in any of the history books because he never existed. Those pictures were faked so that anyone trying to find out what was happening would think there really was an Eerie, Indiana, in the eighteen hundreds."

"Our town founders are from outer space?" said Simon. He sounded like he might faint.

"How did you find all of this out?" I asked Priscilla.

"I have some connections in the government," she said. "A friend of mine is very interested in the unexplained. He works for the FBI, investigating weird stuff. He came across a file that mentioned Eerie, and he suggested that I check it out."

"So the government knows all about Eerie?" I said.

"Some people in the government do," Priscilla answered. "And those people want to make sure that nobody else finds out. That's why they've kept me here."

"We saw Miss Information going through your book with a marker," I said. "She was crossing lots of things out."

Priscilla laughed. "That's all part of their plan," she said. "They're going through my book and getting rid of all the facts. Then they're going to replace all of the facts with lies and publish a new edition of the book. They're going to say that I disappeared because I was rethinking my original theories and decided that I was wrong. The new book will say that all the UFO stories are hoaxes, and people will believe it."

"What about the man in black?" I said. "Who is he?"

"You mean the man in the photographs from Roswell and from Eerie?" said Priscilla. "I don't know who he is. I've never figured that out. All I know is that he's somebody very influential in the government, and his job is to make sure no one finds out about the aliens."

"So who in Eerie is an alien?" said Simon. "Everyone?"

"That's the hard part," said Priscilla. "There's no way to tell. At first I thought that Miss Information, the mayor, and Mr. Radford were all aliens. But now I'm not sure. I think some of them are aliens and some of them are working for the government, helping to keep things quiet."

"Well, now that we've found you, we have the proof we need," I said. "Let's get out of here and we'll go to the police."

Priscilla shook her head. "We can't do that," she said. "If they find out I'm gone, they'll be onto us. They have ways of making people believe what they want them to. If you go telling people this story, they'll all think you're crazy. Besides, I'm sure some members of the police department are in on this."

"So what do we do?" I asked.

"We need to find someone who can help us," she said. "Someone people will listen to. And I think I know just who that is."

"Who's going to believe a story about a town the government created just to hide some aliens that they deny ever existed in the first place?" I said.

"There's a magazine," said Priscilla. "It's called *National Weirdness.*"

"I've seen that at the grocery store," said Simon. "There was a picture of a two-hundred-pound baby on the cover."

"That's the one," said Priscilla.

"But that stuff is all fake," I said. "They make it all up to sell magazines."

"They make up *some* of it," said Priscilla. "But some of it is true. There are some people who work for those magazines who really are interested in exploring the unexplained. They write about the things that no one else believes. Nobody else will publish what they write, so they go to work for those magazines."

"So what do you want us to do, call this magazine and say we have this great story?" I said.

"That's exactly what you're going to do," said Priscilla.

"Why don't we just call your friend in the FBI?"

"We can't risk that," said Priscilla. "He and his partner have enough trouble as it is with the people who don't want them finding out the truth. This would just make things worse. Our best bet is to contact the magazine. Tell whoever you talk to that something really weird is going on here, and that they can be the first ones to cover it. The more people we reach with this story, the better."

"What if they don't believe me?" I said.

"They have to believe you," said Priscilla. "If they don't, I'll be stuck here forever. And now that they know that you're onto them, you'll be next. You can be sure of that."

Simon looked at me. I thought about Radford's call to the mayor. Priscilla was right: They did know about us. And if they'd kidnapped her and held her prisoner for so long, who knew what they'd do to us? Priscilla only knew part of the story of Eerie. We knew a lot more.

"Okay," I said. "We'll contact them. But what about you?"

"I'll be fine," said Priscilla. "You just go find help."

"We can't go back the way we came," I said. "It's locked on that end."

"You can go up," said Priscilla. "Through the crypt."

"But what about Zebediah's body?" said Simon.

"There is no Zebediah Eerie," I said. "He's a fake, just like everything else. I bet his tomb is empty."

"That's right," said Priscilla. "It's actually a hidden stairway. I've seen them use it before. When you go back to the main room, look for a candlestick bolted to the wall. If you pull it, the stairway will appear."

"But what about the door to the crypt?" I said. "Digger locked it from the outside."

"There's another door," said Priscilla. "It's on the back wall of the crypt, and it blends right into the stone. Push on the third stone from the right, two rows up, and it will open."

"Wow," said Simon. "These aliens sure are smart."

"How do you think they've lasted this long without being found?" said Priscilla. "They have a lot of tricks up their sleeves. You'd better be very careful, and always keep your eyes wide open."

"We will," I said. "And we'll be back for you as soon as we can."

"Good luck," she said.

We left Priscilla's cell. I had to climb up on Simon's shoulders in order to reach the Mercantile sign and pull it back down. I watched as the wall slid back into place, sealing her inside again.

"Look for the candlestick," I said. "We need to get out of here fast."

Shining the flashlight on the walls, I moved the beam of light around the room until I found the candlestick. Simon went over and pulled on it. It moved downward, and there was a click, followed by a rumbling sound.

"The ceiling is caving in!" said Simon.

The ceiling was moving, but it wasn't caving in. A part of it was just descending into the room, almost like an elevator. When it reached the floor, we saw that a set of narrow steps had formed. Running up them, we found ourselves emerging from Zebediah's tomb. The lid had slid back, and we were able to jump out of it and into the crypt. As soon as we were out, the lid slid back and I could hear the stairs folding back up.

"Now for that door," I said.

I turned to the back wall and counted three blocks over and two blocks up. Putting my hand on the stone, I pushed as hard as I could. I didn't need to push so hard. The door swung right open so easily that I actually fell outside, landing face first in the grass.

"Nice move," said Simon, walking out behind me and shutting the door.

"Next time you can go first," I said, sitting up.

I looked up at the sky. The moon was high overhead, and the stars were shining brightly.

"I've never been so happy to be outside in a cemetery in the middle of the night," I said.

"What time is it?" asked Simon.

I checked my watch. "Almost midnight," I said. What with all the running around we'd been doing, I hadn't even realized how late it was.

"I don't know how I'm going to be able to make it through school tomorrow," I said. "I wish we could call the magazine right now. Can you imagine what will happen when people find out about this? It will probably be all over the news. We'll be heroes."

"Maybe they'll even make a movie about us," said Simon. "Or a television show."

"That will be the day," I said. "Eerie, Indiana, as a television show. Get real."

We were so busy talking about what might happen when the story of Eerie got out that we didn't notice we were being followed. When two figures jumped out in front of us from behind some gravestones, we were so startled that all we could do was scream. I dropped the flashlight, and it went out.

"Get them!" said a creepy voice in the dark.

The two figures came toward us, their arms out-stretched. They were all dressed in black, and I couldn't see their faces. But I was pretty sure I didn't want to get close enough to find out who they were.

"Run!" I shouted to Simon when I'd gotten my senses back.

I turned around and took off as fast as I could go. I heard Simon behind me, panting as he ran. The two of us had run from a lot of creepy things before, so I knew we could do it again. Or at least I hoped we could.

Because it was dark and I didn't have the flashlight, I didn't really know where I was going. I just ran. I dodged gravestones as they popped up in front of me, jumping over the low ones and running around the high ones. A couple of times I tripped and almost fell, but I managed to get back up and keep going.

As I ran, I could hear several pairs of footsteps behind me. I knew one of them was Simon's. But I knew the others belonged to the creepy figures, and they seemed to be gaining on us.

I realized suddenly that I was running deeper and deeper into the cemetery. If we were caught, there would be no one there to help us. Even worse, I didn't know any way out except through the front gate. All I could do was keep running. My heart was beating heavily in my chest, and my lungs felt like they were on fire. But I had to go on.

As I dashed around a giant monument with angels on either side, I heard a crashing sound behind me. When

I looked over my shoulder, I saw that Simon had fallen on the ground. He was lying on his stomach, trying to get back on his feet. In the darkness behind him, I saw two even darker shadows leaping over tombstones only a few yards away.

"Keep going!" he shouted. "Don't let them catch you."

I turned around and started back toward Simon.

"No!" he said. "Just go."

I knew that if I went back, we might both be caught. But I couldn't let my best friend end up trapped by whatever was chasing us.

"Come on," I said, grabbing his arm and pulling him up. "We can make it."

The figures were gaining on us. I could hear them breathing as I struggled to get Simon to his feet. Finally he was up and ready to run. I turned to go as the first figure made a last-minute jump at us.

I felt a hand close around the back of my shirt. Throwing myself forward, I tried as hard as I could to break free. But it was no use. I'd been caught. I started thrashing around, yelling.

"Let me go!" I shouted. "I haven't done anything."

Beside me, Simon was trying to get away from the second figure, who had him pinned to the ground. He was beating at it with his hands.

The two figures didn't say anything as they wrestled

us under control. Now that I was closer, I could see that they were two men.

"What's the big deal?" I said, still pretending to be innocent. "Can't a guy take a walk in the cemetery without getting jumped on? I have rights, you know."

"Do you now, Mr. Teller?" said the same voice I'd heard commanding the men to grab us. "We'll just have to see about that."

Another figure came walking out of the darkness. I watched as it moved silently between the gravestones, a shadow walking through the night. While I was afraid of the men holding us down, I was even more afraid of whoever or whatever it was that was coming toward me. I tried to look over at Simon, but the man on top of me was pushing me into the grass, and I couldn't turn my head. All I could do was lie there, waiting to see what was coming for me.

Just as the figure was emerging from the darkness, there was an explosion of bright light from somewhere behind me. The area around us was flooded with light, and the figure in front of me threw up its arms to cover its face.

"What are you doing here?" someone shouted. "You leave those boys alone!"

Someone came running up from behind us. The man on top of me stood up suddenly and took off into the darkness. I looked over and saw that Simon, too, was free. I looked for the third figure, but he was also gone. I tried to find them in the blackness, but there was no sign of them.

"Are you okay?" said the new voice. Someone knelt in the grass beside me, and I looked up to see who had rescued us.

"Digger!" I said, looking into his worried face. He was carrying a big flashlight.

"What in blazes are you doing in here at this time of night?" he said, helping me up and then going over to Simon. "And who were those fellows?"

For a minute, I thought about telling Digger the truth. After saving us, he deserved to know. But I didn't want to put him into any more danger than he was already in. Besides, I really didn't know who the men were.

"They just jumped out at us," I said honestly. "I don't know who they were."

Digger made a grunting sound. "That still doesn't explain what you two were doing out here," he said.

I thought hard. "I left something here," I said. "My notebook. When you let us in to see Zebediah's grave, I must have dropped it on the ground."

"So you came all the way back here in the middle of the night for it?" said Digger, looking first at me and then at Simon. "Dressed up like a couple of spies."

I nodded. "I . . . um . . . have a test tomorrow, and I needed my notes to study."

I could tell Digger didn't believe me, but he didn't say anything. He just nodded. "Well, you'd best be leaving now. No telling what else is running around this place. Wouldn't have come out myself except I heard all the ruckus."

"Well, we're glad you did," I said. "Thanks."

"Yeah, thanks," said Simon.

For the second time in as many days, Digger walked us back to the front gate of the cemetery. As we went along, I looked for any signs of the men who had chased us, but they had vanished into the night as though they'd never been there.

"All right, now," said Digger when we reached the gates. "You boys go straight home. And next time you need to come through here, you do it in the daytime, you hear? I might not be around to save your sorry hides again."

"Don't worry," I said. "I don't want to see this place again for a long time."

"Me neither," said Simon.

"Okay, then," he said. "Now get on home."

We started to walk away.

"And kid," Digger said.

I turned around. "Yeah?"

"Good luck on that test, whatever it is. I hope you pass with flying colors."

"Thanks," I said. "So do I."

"*D*o you think they know where we live?" asked Simon as we walked toward home.

"That guy knew my name," I said. "And he probably knows yours. Just to be safe, make sure you lock your door and keep the windows closed."

"This is getting too weird," said Simon. "I mean, we've seen and done some strange things, but we've never had anyone attack us like that. And how did they know we were there?"

"This isn't like anything else we've encountered," I said. "This is big. Really big. And I bet there are a lot of people who don't want us to tell anyone what we know. They might be watching us."

"Maybe we should just forget it," said Simon. He sounded scared. Sometimes I forget that even though he's seen a lot, he's still a kid.

"We can't," I said. "Priscilla is counting on us. Now

let's get home. It's after midnight, and we still have to go to school tomorrow.''

"School," groaned Simon. "How am I supposed to sit through classes after all of this?"

"Hey," I said, "after almost getting caught by Miss Information and the mayor, walking through that tunnel, finding Priscilla, and almost getting kidnapped by who-knows-what, I'll be glad to just sit at a desk all day."

Simon sighed. "I guess when you look at it that way, it's not such a bad idea. Okay, then. I'll see you tomorrow."

"Make sure you wash that black stuff off," I said. "You look like a chimney sweep."

I watched as Simon went into his house, carefully opening the door so he wouldn't wake up his parents. Hopefully, they would think he was already in bed and wouldn't have waited up.

Once he was inside, I went around to the back of my house. The ladder was still hanging from my window, which meant that no one had noticed my disappearance. I climbed back up and into my room. I don't think I've ever been so glad to see my bed as I was then. After everything that had happened, all I wanted to do was go to sleep.

Which is just what I did, as soon as I pulled the ladder back in, shut the window, and made sure my door was locked. If anyone was going to try and get into my room, I wanted to make it as difficult as possible. After I was sure everything was safe, I crawled into bed and fell asleep almost before my head hit the pillow.

The next morning came way too quickly for my liking. When my alarm clock rang, it seemed as though I'd only been asleep for about five minutes. But there it was, seven o'clock, and time to get up and get ready for school. I managed to fall out of bed, take a fast shower to wash off the grass stains from the night before, and find some clothes to wear, but when I went downstairs I was still yawning.

"Up late studying, Marshall?" said my mother. She was popping frozen waffles into the toaster.

"Sure," I said sleepily. I was too tired to make up any good excuses, so I let her think what she wanted to.

"That's my boy," she said. "I'm so glad you're such a responsible young man. I don't have to worry about you sneaking out or getting into trouble or anything."

"Gee, thanks," I said. I wondered what she would think if she knew I'd been running around underground Eerie and almost getting snatched by what were probably aliens.

As I was buttering a piece of toast, my father ran in, trying to tie his tie and find his briefcase at the same time. Grabbing a glass of orange juice from my mother, he almost spilled it all over himself as he attempted to use the same hand to tighten the noose he'd made around his neck.

"Good morning, family," he said. "How is everyone?"

"Fine," I said.

"Great," Dad said. "Now where did I put that project I was working on last night?"

He started rummaging through the refrigerator, pulling out containers of leftovers and opening them. As he opened one and started to sniff it, there was a knock at the back door.

"That must be Paul," he said.

"Who's Paul?" I asked.

"New guy at work," said Dad, taking one of the leftover containers and putting it in his briefcase. "Nice guy. He's giving me a ride to work while the car is in the shop. Would you let him in?"

I went over to the door and opened it. When I saw who was standing there, I nearly dropped my juice. It was one of the men who had tried to capture Simon and me the night before. Only now he was wearing a suit and tie. He just looked at me and smiled as though he'd never seen me before and everything was fine.

I was sure there was some mistake. This guy had somehow turned up at my house at the same time my dad's friend was supposed to. He was going to kidnap me or do something awful to my family. I had to warn them.

But when my dad turned around, he just smiled.

"Hi, Paul," he said, waving him in. "Come on in. I'll be ready in a minute. Everyone, this is Paul Groan."

"It's actually Grohne," the man said. "It's a German name. The e is *not* silent."

Paul walked into the kitchen and looked around. I remembered how his hands had felt holding me down, and I felt my heart racing. I wanted to run out of the room, or tell everyone that the man standing in our house was an alien, or at least working for them. But I didn't say that. What I said was, "Would you like some juice?" I couldn't believe how lame it sounded.

Paul looked at me and smiled, showing his teeth. "No, thank you, Marshall," he said. The way he said my name made chills run up and down my spine. I backed around to the other side of the table and watched him warily. That's when I noticed that he had a big bruise on his cheek. I wondered if he'd gotten it when I was trying to fight him off. I hoped so.

My dad picked up his briefcase and started to leave. Then he saw Paul's face.

"Wow," he said. "That's quite a bruise. What happened to you?"

Paul laughed. "Oh, it was nothing," he said. "I just

89

had a little accident last night. I was trying to catch a rat that had gotten into the cellar, and I tripped over it.''

"Ouch," said Dad. "It must have been one big rat."

"Oh, it was," said Paul, looking at me. "And it got away, too. But it won't be so lucky next time."

Dad chuckled. "Okay, then," he said, oblivious to the fact that I was being threatened in my own kitchen. "We're off to work." He kissed my mother good-bye and headed out.

"Bye, Paul," my mother said. "It was nice to meet you."

"Same to you," he said, waving. "And it was nice to see you, Marshall. I hope we meet again soon."

I managed a half smile. "Sure," I said. "And watch out for those rats."

"Well, wasn't he nice?" my mother said after they were gone. "I hope we get to see more of him."

I didn't say anything as I pulled on my jacket and picked up my backpack. As far as I was concerned, I wished we would never see Paul again. But somehow I didn't think that my wish would come true.

I left the house and met Simon at the corner. As we walked to school, I told him about my dad's new coworker.

"I wonder where the other one will turn up," said Simon. "And there's still the guy who was telling them what to do. We never even saw him, so we won't know him if we run into him.''

"We should be safe at school,'' I said as we walked toward B. F. Skinner Junior High. "What could happen to us there?''

I found out what could happen when I walked into Miss Earhart's history class later that day. Nothing strange had happened all day, and I had actually started to think that things might turn out okay. Then I got to history and found out we had a substitute. A few minutes after I sat down, the door opened and a man walked in. It was the second man from the cemetery.

"Good afternoon,'' he said, standing in front of the blackboard. "I'm Mister Rogers. Miss Earhart called in missing . . . I mean sick . . . this morning, so I'll be taking over the class until she is found, er, feels better.''

He sat down at the desk and looked at the seating chart. Then he looked up and stared right at me.

"Mister Teller,'' he said. "Why don't you tell us what you know about the ancient pyramids of Egypt? That *is* what you were supposed to be doing last night, correct? Reading about the pyramids?''

"Um, I guess so,'' I said. I tried to remember what I knew about the pyramids, but I couldn't think about anything except how Mr. Rogers had looked jumping over tombstones as he chased Simon and me through the graveyard. Now he looked like an ordinary "sub," but the night before he'd been out to get me.

"Do you remember *anything* about the pyramids, Mister Teller?" he said, smiling. "Or maybe you were doing something else last night—something more important."

The whole class laughed as they waited for me to say something. Finally, I said the only thing that came to my mind. "The pyramids were built by aliens," I blurted out. I don't know why I said it. I had read something about it being a possibility in a book once, but I certainly didn't want to say it in front of the whole class.

Mr. Rogers smiled as the class roared with laughter. When they finally quieted down, he folded his hands on the desk in front of him.

"That's quite an interesting theory, Mr. Teller," he said. "Do you think these—these aliens—did anything else we should know about?"

The class burst into giggles. I felt my face turning bright red. He was making me look like a fool. I wanted to stand up and shout, "You know very well what else the aliens have done!" But I knew I couldn't. If I did, I'd never be able to live it down. He had me right where he wanted me.

"I guess not," I mumbled.

For the rest of the hour, Mr. Rogers told us all about

the pyramids in Egypt and how they were built. Normally I would have found the topic fascinating, but I wasn't really listening. I was too scared.

When the bell finally rang and the period was over, I was the first one out the door. I didn't even bother to put my books in my locker. I just ran out the front door and down the steps to meet Simon.

"Come on," I said. "We don't have any time to lose. They're all around us."

I practically ran home as Simon jogged along behind me, trying to keep up. I kept looking behind me, expecting to see the two men chasing us, but there was no one there. Still, I didn't want to take any chances.

When we reached my house, I went inside and locked the door behind us. Then we ran up to my room and shut the door.

"So, what are we doing?" said Simon.

"We're calling *National Weirdness,*" I said.

I reached under my bed and pulled out a box. I opened the top and started looking through what was inside. Mostly it was just comic books, but underneath them were some magazines that I kept out of sight so my mom wouldn't find them if she ever decided to clean under there.

"Here it is," I said, pulling out a copy of *National Weirdness.* "I bought this because there was an article in it about some kids who claimed all the exchange students in their school were really blue lizards from Venus.''

I flipped to the front of the magazine. "Here's the phone number of their office," I said. "Hand me the phone."

Simon picked up the phone from my desk and gave it to me.

"What are you going to say?" he asked.

I started to dial the number. "I'm not sure," I said.

The phone rang five times before someone finally picked it up.

"Hello," said a woman's voice. *"National Weirdness."*

"Um, hi," I said, feeling really stupid.

"Can I help you?" said the woman.

"I don't know," I said. "I have a weird story to report."

The woman sighed. "You and everyone else on the planet," she said. "What is it this time? You think there's a monster under the bed? Your parents are really zombies? What?"

"No," I said. "It's a story about aliens."

"Oh, great," said the woman. "Let me guess, you think you were abducted by aliens."

"Well, we almost were," I said. "But that's not it. See, our town was founded to hide aliens. The aliens from Roswell, New Mexico."

There was silence on the other end. Then the woman came back on the line. This time, she sounded serious.

"Did you say Roswell?"

"Yes," I said. "I live in Eerie, Indiana, and—"

"Just a minute," she said, interrupting me. "I'm going to connect you with someone who can help you."

There was a pause as the phone clicked a few times. Then someone else picked up.

"This is Maury Rivera," said a man's voice. "You have some information about the Roswell aliens?"

"That's right," I said.

"I'm listening," he said. "Start talking."

10

"Well, Mr. Rivera," I began. "This is going to sound really weird."

He snorted. "Kid, I've heard every weird story in the book. This one can't be any weirder than the rest of them."

"Okay. Well, I live in a town called Eerie, Indiana," I said. "A lot of strange stuff happens here."

"Get to the point," said Maury Rivera irritably. "I haven't got all day. What does this have to do with Roswell?"

"I think our town was founded as a place to hide the aliens from Roswell," I said in a rush. I didn't want him to hang up on me. "I think maybe our mayor is an alien, and a lot of other people, too. They've kidnapped a woman named Priscilla Bartlett, and . . ."

"Wait a minute," said Mr. Rivera. "Did you say Priscilla Bartlett? You mean the author who disappeared earlier this year?"

"That's her," I said. "They have her locked up in a secret room."

"You found her? And she told you all of this—about the Roswell aliens and everything?"

"Well, part of it," I said. "A lot of it I figured out on my own. Me and my friend Simon, anyway. See, I started to research my town's history, and I found these photos that—"

"This is a great story," said Mr. Rivera. I felt as if everyone I talked to at *National Weirdness* was only interested in interrupting me. But at least he seemed to be listening.

"Do you think you'd like to do a story about it?" I asked.

"I'll do even better, kid," he said. "I'll be there on the next plane out of here. Then you can tell me the story in person."

"That's great!" I said. "We have photos and everything. This will be the best story ever."

"I can be there by eight o'clock," said Mr. Rivera. "Just tell me where to meet you and your friend."

I tried to think of a good place to meet him, someplace where no one would see us and suspect anything. "Meet us at the abandoned mill," I said. "It's on Route Thirteen right outside of town. You can't miss it."

"I'll be there," he said. "By the way, who else have you told about this?"

"No one," I said. "Just you."

"That's perfect," he said. "Make sure you keep this a secret. Don't tell anybody. We wouldn't want anyone to ruin our story."

"Got it," I said. "We won't tell a soul."

Maury Rivera hung up. I put the phone back and sat down on my bed.

"He says he'll be here at eight," I told Simon.

"I can't believe this," said Simon. "Finally someone is going to listen to what we have to say. This is what we've been waiting for."

"I know," I said. I thought it was kind of strange that Mr. Rivera believed everything I was telling him so easily, and that he could get to Eerie so quickly, but I figured he dealt with this kind of stuff all the time, so he knew what he was doing.

"What should we do until eight?" said Simon.

"Let's put together a file with everything we know and everything we've collected so far about the aliens," I said. "That way we'll have something to show Mr. Rivera tonight."

For the next few hours, Simon and I wrote down everything that had happened since the day we'd first gone inside the town hall to find out about Zebediah Eerie. There was a lot to say, and I didn't want to leave anything out. I also put into the file the copies of the pictures that Mrs. Ghostley had in her collection. When we were finally finished, the folder was pretty thick.

"This should really impress him," I said.

"I hope so," said Simon. "Hey, maybe he'll even give us jobs working for *National Weirdness.* We could write about all the creepy stuff we see around here."

"We'll see," I said, putting the file into my backpack. "Right now it's time to get over to the mill and wait for Mr. Rivera."

We told my mother that I was eating over at Simon's. Then Simon called his mother and told her that he was eating over at our house. We got on our bikes and rode through town and out past the cemetery on Route 13. As we rode, I kept my eyes open for any sign of Mr. Grohne and Mr. Rogers. If they were following us, they were doing a great job of staying invisible, because I never saw them.

At about seven-thirty we came to the old mill. It sat a little ways away from the main road, down a dirt lane and next to the river. At one time the mill had been used to saw trees for lumber, but there had been a mysterious accident, and a logger was beheaded by a saw. After that, people said his headless ghost haunted the mill, and no one would work there. It had been shut down, and now it just sat there falling apart. Simon and I had once spent the night in the mill, hoping to see the ghost, but he never appeared.

We parked our bikes at the side of the road and sat under some big elm trees to wait for Mr. Rivera. It was just starting to get dark, and the bugs were chirping all around us. I thought about Priscilla sitting underground in her dark cell and hoped we would be able to rescue her soon.

A few minutes before eight, I saw headlights approaching on the road.

"Hide in the bushes," I said to Simon. "If it isn't Mr. Rivera, we don't want whoever it is to see us."

The two of us pushed our bikes into the tall weeds that surrounded the mill. We were still able to see out, but if anyone came by, they wouldn't be able to see us. We crouched down in the grass and watched the road.

The headlights stopped at the dirt road and turned in. We stayed hidden as the car pulled up beside the mill and stopped. The lights went out, and the door opened. Someone got out and started looking around.

"Where are those kids?" said a gruff voice. "I better not have come all the way out here for nothing."

"That's him," I whispered to Simon. "I recognize his voice. Come on."

We came out of the bushes and walked toward the car.

"Mr. Rivera?" I said.

The man jumped. "Don't scare me like that," he said. "What were you doing in there?"

"We wanted to make sure it was you," I said.

"We've had a little trouble with people trying to get us."

"I know how that can be," said Mr. Rivera. "You must be Marshall."

"That's right," I said. "And this is Simon."

"You guys look a little young to be playing detective," he said.

"It just sort of happened," I said. "This place has a way of dragging you into stuff, whether you like it or not."

Mr. Rivera looked just like I thought he would. He was tall, and he was wearing wrinkled clothes, like he'd slept in them the night before or something. His hair was kind of a mess, and he had on sneakers. He looked like I always thought newspaper reporters must look.

"We made this for you," I said, taking the folder out of my backpack and handing it to him. "It's all the information we have."

He opened the folder and looked through it. As he read what Simon and I had written, he nodded his head. A couple of times he grunted.

"Good work, boys," he said after he'd leafed through most of it. "You two seem to know a lot about what's going on in this town. Now, what exactly did Priscilla Bartlett tell you about Eerie?" asked Mr. Rivera.

"She said that the government invented Eerie as a place to hide the aliens that had been captured at Roswell," I said. "We couldn't believe they would just invent a town, but it sure looks that way."

"The government can do anything it wants to," said Mr. Rivera. "They can invent towns and make them disappear again. Same with people. Or aliens."

"Do you really think there are aliens in Eerie?" I asked.

He shook his head. "There could be," he said. "We won't really know for sure until we look around some more."

I liked the way Mr. Rivera said "we," as though we were a team now. He paused for a moment, then he said, "Did Priscilla Bartlett tell you why she thought so many other weird things happened in Eerie?"

I shook my head. "No," I said. "We know Eerie is shaped like the Bermuda Triangle, but we don't really know what that has to do with the aliens or anything. That was going to be the next part of our investigation."

Mr. Rivera took a pen out of his pocket and wrote something in the folder. "There are a lot of people who wish Priscilla Bartlett would just disappear forever," he said. "You're probably the only two who know she's still alive. Did you tell anyone else about her?"

"No," I said. "No one would believe us, anyway."

"That's good," he said. "Very good."

"We *are* going to rescue her, aren't we?" said Simon.

Mr. Rivera smiled. "That would be a big story, wouldn't it?" he said. "Then she could reveal everything she knows about Eerie, and everybody would know."

"Who do you think the guys are who keep trying to catch us?" I asked. "One of them works with my dad, and the other one is a substitute teacher at school."

"I don't know," said Mr. Rivera. "They could be aliens, or they could just work for them. It's hard to say. Didn't you say there was a third man?"

"Yes," I said. "But we've never seen his face, so we don't know what he looks like."

Mr. Rivera made another note in the folder. "Excellent," he said. "That's very good to know."

"So what happens now?" I asked.

"I think we should take Simon's advice and rescue Priscilla," said Mr. Rivera. "With what you know and what she knows, we can blow the lid right off this story. By next week, everyone will know what's going on in Eerie, Indiana."

"Great," I said. "I knew calling you was the right thing to do. I knew you'd be on my side."

"Sure I am, kid," said Mr. Rivera. "Sure I am."

He looked at his watch. "Look, it's getting late. I have to go meet some people . . . I mean, get something to eat. Why don't you boys meet me at midnight at Zebediah Eerie's crypt? Then we can put this plan into action."

"We'll be there," I said. "You can count on it."

"Okay," he said. "I'll leave here first. That way, if anyone is following me, they'll follow the car and you two can get out of here safely."

"Got it," I said. "We'll see you at midnight, then."

Mr. Rivera opened the car door and started to get in.

"Mr. Rivera?" I said.

"What, kid?"

"Thanks for coming."

"Oh, it's my pleasure," he said. "I wouldn't miss this for the world."

He shut the car door and started the engine. Without turning his headlights on, he backed out onto the main road. Then he flicked the lights on and drove away. Simon and I waited a few minutes to make sure no other cars were following him. Then we got on our bikes and rode away from the mill.

"Wasn't he great?" I said to Simon as we pedaled back into town. "A real reporter."

"Yeah," said Simon. "This is going to be really great. Just think, we're going to be responsible for exposing one of the biggest government cover-ups of all time."

"Now maybe my mom won't think I'm such a space case," I said. "She still thinks I'm acting weird because we had to move away from New Jersey."

"Right," said Simon. "Now she'll know it's because we live in an alien town. I'm sure that will make her feel *much* better."

"Once we get into that crypt it will all be over," I said.

Simon braked his bike to a stop. "Wait a minute," he said. "We never told Mr. Rivera that Priscilla Bartlett was being held underneath Zebediah's crypt. How did he know that?"

"Maybe he read it in the report we wrote," I said. "Don't worry about it."

"I guess you're right," said Simon. We started riding again, and soon we were back home.

"Okay," I said when we reached our houses. "You know what to do. Sneak out and meet me here at eleven-thirty. Then we'll go to the cemetery."

When I got home, my parents were sitting in the living room watching the evening news. The newscaster was talking about the appearance of blue lights over Eerie.

"That's the fifth time this month that we've had one of those meteor showers," said my dad. "That's just amazing."

I needed to get ready for the big meeting with Maury Rivera so I told my parents I was going up to bed.

"Good night, Mars," said my dad. "Keep up the good work, son. Make me proud."

"Oh, I plan on it," I said as I went up the stairs to the Secret Spot.

11

Waiting for the time to pass until I was supposed to meet Simon and go to the cemetery was the hardest thing I'd ever had to do. I looked at the notebooks of information Simon and I had gathered about Eerie. I thought about all of the strange things I'd seen since moving there. Maybe now I would finally find out what it was all about. Once Priscilla was freed, we would unlock the mystery of the Eerie Triangle once and for all.

Finally, it was time to leave. I'd heard my parents go to bed about half an hour before, so I didn't have to worry about them seeing me. Getting out of the house was as simple as throwing the rope ladder out the window and climbing down.

When I got outside, Simon wasn't there. I checked my watch. We only had twenty minutes to get to the cemetery. If he was late, then we wouldn't make it on time. I didn't want Mr. Rivera to think we'd stood him up.

Just as I was thinking I might have to leave without him, Simon came out.

"Sorry I'm late," he said. "My dad was watching a ball game on TV and I couldn't sneak past him. I had to wait until he fell asleep in his chair."

"We'll have to ride hard," I said. "We only have fifteen minutes now to get there."

We hopped on our bikes and made it across town in record time, probably because we were so excited about what was going to happen. In only a few short minutes, it would all be over. The aliens' secret would be revealed, and it would all be because of us.

When we reached the cemetery gates, we parked the bikes in the bushes and climbed over the tall fence. I almost got stuck on the sharp points at the top of the fence posts, but Simon helped push me over, and soon we were standing on the other side.

When we reached the crypt I saw Mr. Rivera leaning up against it, smoking a cigarette.

"What are you doing?" I asked. "What if someone sees you?"

"Don't worry about that," he said, rubbing the cigarette out with his shoe. "No one will bother us."

"How do you know that?" asked Simon.

"It's my job to know things like that," he said. "Now, let's get going."

He walked over to the door and turned the handle.

"Digger locks it," I said. "You can't get in that way."

"Sure I can," he said. He took something out of his pocket and put it into the lock on the door. After a few moments of turning it around, I heard a clicking sound.

"Bingo," said Mr. Rivera. "We're in."

He pushed the door and it swung open.

"How'd you do that?" I asked.

He laughed. "I've learned a few things over the years," he said.

We went into the crypt and Mr. Rivera shut the door behind us. Then he turned on his flashlight and shined it around.

"Nice place," he said jokingly. "It could use some redecorating, though."

"The stairs are under the tomb," I said. "I think if we can slide the top off it will activate them."

The three of us went over to Zebediah's stone coffin. Leaning against the lid, we pushed as hard as we could. There was a slight scraping sound as the stone moved a little.

"Push harder," said Mr. Rivera. "It's starting to give."

Using all of my strength, I shoved the lid of the coffin. Very slowly, it slid aside, until it was almost all of the way off the box. Then it stopped, and I heard a grinding sound begin.

"Those are the stairs," I said. "It's working."

Mr. Rivera shined his flashlight into the opening. We watched as the bottom of the coffin dropped away, becoming the first set of stairs. Slowly the entire stairwell descended into the darkness until we heard it touch the bottom and stop.

"That's amazing!" said Mr. Rivera, leaning over and looking down into the hole.

"Not as amazing as what's down here," I said, climbing over the edge of the tomb. "Follow me."

Mr. Rivera and Simon came after me as I walked down the stairs and into the room beneath the crypt. Everything looked exactly as it had the last time I'd been in there.

"Where's Priscilla Bartlett?" he said. "I thought you told me she was down here."

"She is," I said, pointing to the wall. "Behind there."

I went over to the Eerie Mercantile sign and pulled it. Just as before, the sign slid up the wall, revealing the hidden chamber behind it. Priscilla Bartlett was sitting on the bed. Only this time, her hands were tied behind her back and her mouth was gagged.

When she saw me standing there, Priscilla began to thrash around on the bed, kicking her feet and shaking her head. Simon and I ran over to her and tried to calm her down. I pulled the gag out of her mouth.

"It's okay," I said. "We're here to rescue you. We brought help."

Priscilla was panting. "No," she said. "It's a trap. You have to get out of here."

"What do you mean?" I said. "How would they know we're here?"

"Because I told them," said Mr. Rivera from behind me.

I spun around and stared at him. He was standing in the middle of the doorway, his hands on his hips. He was smiling, but he didn't look at all friendly.

"What do you mean you told them?" I said.

"It's like I told you, kid," he said. "I've learned a thing or two working in this business. One of the most important things I've learned is to make sure you know whose side to be on."

"I don't understand," I said.

"He's working for them," said Priscilla. "He may even *be* one of them. When they came here earlier tonight they said one of their people was taking care of you two. My guess is that he's been in on this from the beginning. I'm so sorry I suggested you call him."

"I knew something was up when he knew about the crypt," said Simon. "But why are you doing this?"

"We'll talk about that later," said Mr. Rivera. He was moving slowly toward us. "Right now I'm going to make sure the two of you stay right here until my friends arrive.''

He lunged at us, trying to grab us. I dodged out of the way, and he stumbled forward.

"Get out of here!" I shouted at Simon.

He ran past Mr. Rivera and managed to get out of the cell and into the main room. But before I could follow him, Mr. Rivera turned back toward me and blocked my way out.

"You're not going anywhere!" he said.

There was no way for me to get out. I was trapped. Mr. Rivera was coming toward me, backing me into the corner. He was getting closer and closer as I tried to think of something—anything—that would get me out of that room. But it was too late. He had me.

Just as Mr. Rivera was reaching for me, Priscilla rolled off the bed and kicked her feet at him. He tripped over her and fell with a thud onto the stone floor.

"Go!" she screamed at me. "Before he gets up!"

"I can't leave you here again," I said.

I ran over and tried to help her up, but her hands were still tied and Mr. Rivera was sprawled across her legs. She couldn't move.

"Just go," she said. "If you don't, they'll have all of us."

Mr. Rivera groaned and opened his eyes.

"He's waking up," said Priscilla. "You don't have any time."

Mr. Rivera started to sit up.

"We'll get you free yet," I said to Priscilla as I stood up and dashed out of the room.

Mr. Rivera was on his hands and knees now, and he was starting to stand up.

"Pull the sign down!" I said to Simon. "We have to shut the door."

I climbed on top of Simon and pulled on the Eerie Mercantile sign. It started to descend, but I wasn't sure it would make it in time. Mr. Rivera was crawling toward the door as Priscilla tried to stop him.

"Come on, come on," I said to myself, willing the sign to move faster. It seemed to be going in slow motion.

My eyes kept going from the sign to Mr. Rivera. He was almost at the door, despite Priscilla's attempts to hold him back. His hand was reaching out.

The door slipped shut just as he was reaching through to try and block it. For a second, his arm was stuck beneath it, but he pulled it away at the last moment. There was a thud as the door closed for good, and I could hear Mr. Rivera banging on it and cursing.

"That should hold him for a while," I said to Simon. "He can't open it from the inside."

"But Priscilla is in there with him," said Simon. "Will she be okay?"

"I hope so," I said. "I don't think they'll hurt her as long as we're still out here. We know too much."

"So what do we do now?" said Simon.

The truth was, I really didn't know what to do next. Mr. Rivera had been my one hope of exposing the alien plot. Now that he couldn't be trusted, I didn't know who else to turn to. It looked like, once again, we were on our own.

"Maybe Digger can help," said Simon. "He lives in the house at the edge of the cemetery."

"It's our only chance," I said. "Let's go."

We started up the stone staircase into Zebediah's crypt. We were just climbing out of the tomb when we heard voices at the door.

"Rivera said they'd be here," said a man who sounded an awful lot like Mr. Rogers. "He should have them under control by now."

"I can't wait to get my hands on those kids," said another man, who I guessed was Mr. Grohne. "They've caused us more problems in one week than we've had in almost fifty years."

"Yeah," agreed Mr. Rogers. "But once Specter gets through with them, they won't be a problem anymore."

I didn't know who Specter was, but the way the two men laughed after they said it made my blood run cold.

"We have to go back down," I whispered to Simon. "There's no time to use the secret door."

We ducked back inside the tomb just as the two men opened the front door and came in. Moving as quickly as we could, we scuttled down the stairs and into the main room. Mr. Rivera was still hitting his fists against the door.

"What now?" said Simon.

Above us, I could hear the men climbing into the coffin and starting down the stairs.

"Get under the clothes," I said to Simon. "Quick."

We ran to the pile of clothing scattered in one corner of the room and dove underneath the mass of coats and dresses only seconds before Mr. Rogers and Mr. Grohne came into the room. Peering out from beneath the edge of a ruffled skirt, I watched them.

"Hey, what's going on here?" said Mr. Rogers. "Where are they?"

The banging on the hidden door grew louder as Mr. Rivera heard the men's voices. Mr. Grohne went and lifted up the Eerie Mercantile sign.

"What happened to you?" he said when the door opened and he saw Mr. Rivera sitting on the floor.

"Those kids got away," he said angrily.

Mr. Rogers snorted. "You couldn't even handle two kids?" he said. "Specter isn't going to be happy about this. Not at all."

"Where did they go?" asked Mr. Grohne.

"I don't know," said Mr. Rivera. "Probably back up those stairs. Didn't you see them?"

"They didn't come out of the crypt," said Mr. Rogers.

"They must have gone back down that way," said Mr. Grohne, pointing to the tunnel entrance. "That means they'll be headed right for the town hall. That's perfect. It's exactly where we want them, anyway. If we hurry, I bet we can get there before the fun begins."

"And at least we still have her," said Mr. Rogers, nodding at Priscilla. "Bring her with us."

The four of them went down the stairs and into the tunnel. Mr. Grohne was pushing Priscilla ahead of him. When I couldn't hear their voices anymore, I pushed the clothes off of me.

"Boy, am I glad to be out from under there," said Simon. "All that dust was making me have to sneeze."

"Well, it's a good thing you didn't," I said, "or they would have had us."

"What do you think he meant when he said they wanted us to go to the town hall?" said Simon. "What's going on there?"

"I'm not sure," I said as I started for the stairs up to the crypt. "But we're going to find out, because that's exactly where we're going."

12

Thankfully, our bikes were still at the cemetery gate when we got there. We jumped on them and tore off down the road, headed for the town hall. I didn't know what was going to happen when we got there, but I knew that if we were going to save Priscilla and find out exactly what was going on in Eerie, we had to get there as quickly as possible. It wouldn't take very long for the men to get through the tunnel, and I wanted to be there first. I couldn't even think about what sort of danger we were getting into. All I could do was pedal.

When we turned onto Main Street, I could barely breathe. But somehow I managed to keep riding until we reached the statue of Zebediah Eerie. Leaving our bikes in the grass, Simon and I raced around the building until we came to the cellar window. Apparently no one had noticed that it was broken, because it was still open. Just as I had the first time, I slipped inside and dropped to the floor. Simon followed right behind me.

"What are we going to do?" he said.

"I have no idea," I answered as I made my way through the basement. "I'm making this up as I go along."

"That makes me feel a *lot* better," said Simon.

We went up the stairs and into the hallway. I could hear the murmur of voices coming from down the hall, but I couldn't make out what was being said.

"That's coming from the direction of the information office," I said. "I bet whoever is here is inside there."

We crept quietly down the hall toward the office. I didn't know how much longer it would be before Mr. Rogers and Mr. Grohne made it through the tunnel with Mr. Rivera and Priscilla Bartlett, but I knew we had to find out what was going on before that happened.

As we approached the office door, the voices grew louder and louder. Whoever was inside was very excited.

"It's not my fault they found out," said a woman's voice. "I don't know how they discovered the way into the tunnel."

"It doesn't matter now, does it?" said a man. "We'll just have to take care of it so they don't tell anyone else."

"It's Miss Information," I said to Simon. "And that voice belongs to the man from the cemetery."

"But who is it?" said Simon.

We got on our hands and knees and crawled to the door, staying down so that no one could see our shadows through the glass. When we were right next to it, I sat up and looked through the keyhole. Inside the room I saw Miss Information sitting at her desk. The man she was talking to was sitting in a chair across from her, and I couldn't see anything but his back.

"What will we do with them?" asked Miss Information.

The man laughed. "Oh, the usual," he said.

"They're talking about us," said Simon. "They're going to do something horrible to us, I just know it. Let's just get out of here."

"We can't," I said. "Priscilla still needs our help. Besides, I want to know what's going on here. We've come this far—we can't back down now, right?"

Simon didn't answer me.

"Right?" I said again. "Don't you want to know what's . . ."

I turned around as I was talking, but I didn't finish my sentence. Standing behind me was a man, and he was holding Simon by the collar. Simon's mouth was hanging open in surprise.

"Uh—oh," was all I managed to say before the man reached down with his free hand and grabbed me, too. Then he opened the door with his foot and pushed us through.

"Hey, boss," he said. "Look what I found sitting outside the door."

The man in the chair turned around to look at us. When I saw his face, I knew we were in trouble. Big trouble. It was the man in the black suit from the photographs.

"Well, well, well," he said when he saw us, just like the villain in a movie. "Look what we have here."

He got up and walked over to us. I saw that he was wearing the same suit he had on in the two photos. I wondered if it was the only one he had.

"Who are you?" I said.

The man raised one eyebrow. "You're asking *me* questions?" he said. "Don't you think it should be the other way around?"

"Why?" I said. "You probably know everything anyway."

The man laughed again. "That's right," he said. "I do. So why don't we just wait for our friends to arrive? Then we can get this over with."

The man who had captured us pushed us toward the chairs in the corner and sat us down roughly. The man in the black suit returned to his chair, and Miss Information looked at us from behind her desk.

A few minutes later, there was a buzzing sound from the phone on the desk.

"They're here," said Miss Information.

She picked up the phone and hit the button to activate the secret entrance. We watched as the file cabinets slid back and the steps appeared. Then Mr. Rogers came up them, shoving Priscilla Bartlett into the office. He was followed by Mr. Grohne and Mr. Rivera.

"I don't know where those kids went," said Mr. Rogers. "We didn't see them in the tunnel."

The man in black smiled. "Why, they're right here," he said, gesturing toward us.

Mr. Rogers turned around and saw us. "But how did they get out without our seeing them?" he stammered.

"I guess they're just smarter than you are," said the man in black.

Mr. Rogers scowled. "I'll enjoy taking care of those two," he said. "They've been nothing but trouble."

"Later," said the man in black. "First let us attend to the young lady."

He walked over to Priscilla.

"I've been waiting a long time to meet you," he said. "I read your book. I found it very . . . interesting."

He looked at Simon and me, and then at Priscilla.

"My name is Specter," he said. "Oliver A. Specter, to be exact. I work for certain . . . interested parties . . . who like to keep an eye on what's happening in this town."

"You mean the government," said Priscilla.

"You mean the aliens," I said.

Specter smiled. "You're both right," he said. "As you seem to have found out, Eerie, Indiana, is the home of some of the Roswell aliens."

"Some of them?" I said. "You mean there are more someplace else?"

"Perhaps," said Specter. "Perhaps not. I'm not at liberty to tell you that. All I will say is that after news of what happened at Roswell leaked out, I was made responsible for looking after our alien friends."

"But why here?" said Simon.

"Because no one would think to look here," said Specter. "Look at this place—it's the most normal town in the whole United States. Why, it could be any town in any state. In fact, it's so normal that no one even noticed when we came in and built a town almost overnight."

"That's why so many weird things happen here, isn't it?" I said. "The weirdness is attracted to Eerie because of the aliens."

Specter laughed. "It's not quite as simple as that," he said.

"What do you mean?" I said.

"I suppose some weird things *do* come here all on their own," he said. "But most of them are put here."

"Put here?" said Simon. "By who?"

"Who do you think?" said Specter. "By the government."

"I don't get it," I said. "I understand hiding the aliens here, but why all this other stuff?"

Specter sighed. "Do I really have to explain that?"

I nodded. So did Simon and Priscilla.

"There are many, many, shall we say . . . peculiar . . . things in the world," said Specter. "If ordinary people knew about them, they would be very upset. So there are people, such as myself, whose job it is to go out and find these things. Then we put them where no one will stumble upon them accidentally. Where they will be out of the way."

"You mean Eerie is sort of a . . . a zoo, for everything weird that you find?" I said.

"Something like that," said Specter. "We prefer to think of it as containing the weirdness in one spot."

"So you know about every strange thing in Eerie?" said Simon.

Specter looked down. "Not exactly," he said.

"What do you mean 'not exactly'?" I said.

"About thirty years ago," he said, "we discovered that things had gotten a little bit out of control in Eerie. Things we hadn't brought here began to pop up all on their own. Odd sightings were reported."

"Why did that happen?" I asked.

"We don't really know," said Specter. "Probably for the same reason that things grew out of control in Atlantis and then in the Bermuda Triangle. The weirdness

122

began to attract other weirdness, and pretty soon no one knew what was happening."

"So you have no way of knowing exactly what's out there?" I said.

Specter stared at me for a minute without speaking. He didn't look happy. "No," he said finally. "We don't."

"Great," said Simon. "Even the government has no idea what's going on."

"Does that surprise you?" said Priscilla, and Specter scowled at her.

"What does he have to do with it?" I asked, nodding my head toward Mr. Rivera.

"Ah, Mr. Rivera," said Specter. "He plays a very interesting part in all of this. You see, *National Weirdness* is a government publication."

"What?" said Simon, Priscilla, and I all at the same time.

"But I thought you wanted to keep this all a secret," I added.

"You can't keep *everything* a secret," said Specter. "If you do, then people get suspicious. We simply publish half-truths, enough of the story to make people think they know something, but not enough for them to know the truth."

"No wonder you came out here so fast when I called," I said to Mr. Rivera. "You weren't after a story at all. You were after me. You probably knew all along what's been going on here.''

"Sorry, kid," said Mr. Rivera. "A guy has to make a living. I just needed to find out exactly what you knew and make sure you didn't tell anyone else.''

"So now what are you going to do with us?" I said to Specter.

He shook his head. "That *is* a problem, isn't it?" he said. "The three of you could cause a great deal of trouble for me—for all of us. I can't let that happen.''

He looked at Priscilla. "As you know," he said. "Miss Information here has been working on a new edition of your book. We are almost finished with that, and it should be in stores early next year. Hopefully, that will undo some of what your snooping around has done. In fact, we expect it to be a best-seller. As for what we will do with you, I think we will give you a new identity. Then we will erase what you know about us from your mind, and you will start life over again somewhere new. You won't even remember that any of this happened.''

"You can't do that!" said Priscilla.

"Certainly we can," said Specter. "The alien technology is quite advanced. How do you think I've managed to stay looking so young for so long?''

"I thought it might be Foreverware," said Simon.

"What?" said Specter.

"Never mind," I said. "It's a long story. You don't want to hear it."

"Well, as for you two," Specter continued, "I think perhaps erasing your memories would be a good idea, too. But we wouldn't want you to disappear and raise any suspicions, so we'll leave you right here in Eerie. Once you've forgotten what you know, you'll fit in just fine with everyone else."

He turned to Mr. Rogers and Mr. Grohne.

"Why don't you put them in the car and take them to the control center," he said. "The technician will be waiting to take care of them."

The two men came toward us.

"Wait!" I shouted. "Can't we make a deal?"

Specter laughed loudly. "A deal?" he said. "Why would I make a deal with you?"

"Because if you don't, I'll expose your entire operation," I said.

"And just how would you do that with no memories?" said Specter.

"Someone else knows about you," I said. "Before we went to meet Mr. Rivera, I made a copy of all the information Simon and I have about what's been going on here in Eerie. I mailed it to someone—someone who will make sure the whole world knows if anything happens to us. Anything at all. In fact, he's going to write a book about it and everyone will read it."

Specter stood up. His face was red. "You're bluffing," he said. "You wouldn't do that."

"Yes, he would," said Simon. "You don't know him."

"Tell me who you sent it to," said Specter.

"No," I said, staring him down. My heart was beating a mile a minute, and I knew I was starting to sweat.

"If you don't," he said. "I'll make sure you don't remember anything ever again."

"Go ahead," I said. "I'd love to forget about this creepy place and not have to worry about getting chased by aliens or meeting up with ghosts. You're the one with everything to lose."

For another minute, Specter stared into my eyes. I didn't blink.

"All right," he said finally. "What's your deal?"

"Well," I said. "You admit that you don't know everything weird about Eerie, right?"

Specter nodded.

"Okay. Well, Simon and I know a lot. For whatever reason, we keep running across the weirdness in Eerie. And we keep records of everything we find."

"So what?" said Specter. "We already know that."

"Yeah," I said. "But don't you see? We see stuff that you don't. I mean, we were the first ones in fifty years to figure you out, right? We can be scouts for you. Whenever we find something weird, we make a

126

report about it. That way, you know what's happening here."

Specter rubbed his chin. "You might have a point there," he said. "It would be nice to know what's going on here. I can't be everywhere at once."

"Exactly," I said. "So, do we have a deal?"

"Don't trust him, boss," said Mr. Rogers.

Specter glared at him. "You be quiet," he said. "He managed to pull one over on you, didn't he?"

Specter looked thoughtful for a minute. "All right," he said finally. "I'll let you go."

"Priscilla too," I said.

Specter grimaced. "The woman, too," he said. "But in exchange, she promises not to write her new book, and you will promise never to reveal what you know to anyone else. If you do, I will come back for you. And next time, I won't be so pleasant."

I looked at Simon and Priscilla. They nodded.

"Deal," I said.

"Very well, then," said Specter. "You may go. I must say, I am impressed with you, Mr. Teller."

"Hey," I said. "It's all in a day's work."

We started to leave, but I thought of something. "One last thing," I said to Specter. "Are Mayor Chisel and Mr. Radford really aliens?"

Specter grinned. "Maybe that should be the first riddle you try to solve," he said.

EPILOGUE

When I woke up the next day, I was exhausted but happy. Sure, I'd only solved part of the mystery of Eerie, Indiana. But I had to hand it to myself—I'd done a pretty good job of bluffing my way out of trouble. And to tell the truth, it was kind of exciting, knowing that there were aliens in my town who were responsible for things as cool as the Bermuda Triangle and Atlantis. As I got ready for school, I wondered if I would ever really know everything there was to know about Eerie and the weirdness in it.

Simon and I talked about everything except the aliens as we walked to school. I think we both wanted to believe that everything was back to normal, or at least as normal as life could be in Eerie. When we passed the statue of Zebediah, we didn't even mention it.

When it was time for history class I was actually looking forward to seeing Miss Earhart again. I pushed open the door and walked in whistling, just happy to be there. I looked up to say hello to Miss Earhart.

And I dropped my books on the floor.

Standing behind Miss Earhart's desk, writing on the board, was Priscilla Bartlett. When she heard me drop my books, she turned around.

"Are you okay?" she asked.

"I'm—um—fine," I said, gathering up my books. Then I went over to her and whispered, "What are you doing here? I thought you were leaving."

"Leaving?" she said, a confused look on her face. "Why would I leave Eerie? It's the most beautiful place I've ever been."

Priscilla was looking at me strangely. Her eyes seemed empty, as though she didn't even recognize me.

"Priscilla?" I said.

She wrinkled her forehead. "Priscilla?" she said. "My name isn't Priscilla. It's Miss Jenkins. Sheila Jenkins. Miss Earhart was . . . called away suddenly. I'm your new history teacher."

Suddenly I realized that Priscilla didn't recognize me. She didn't remember anything from the night before. She didn't even know who she was. The aliens had drained her memories after all. They must have gotten her after Simon and I left.

"Okay, class," said Priscilla when the bell rang. "Today we're going to talk about something special. I think you'll all find it very interesting."

She picked a pile of books off her desk and started

walking down the aisles, handing them out. She dropped one on my desk with a sickening plop. I picked it up and looked at the cover.

The History of Eerie: The Revised Edition it said, by Oliver A. Specter.

*T*he weirdness started when I was getting ready to go on my paper route. I don't like to leave the house unless I'm wearing my favorite sneakers. They're old and kind of battered, but they fit my feet perfectly. And that morning they weren't where I'd left them, next to my bed.

Mom had bought me a brand-new pair two weeks earlier. They were okay, but needed some serious wearing in. I figured that my missing sneakers were Mom's way of telling me to accelerate the wearing-in program.

"Have you seen my old sneakers?" I asked her when I went downstairs.

"Not since yesterday," Mom answered cheerfully.

"When you were still wearing them. Aren't you ever going to use that nice new pair I bought you?"

I turned to my older sister Syndi. "Did you move them?"

"As if I'd touch your ratty old sneakers," she said with a sniff. "You probably just lost them."

"I never lose things," I told her. I went to look for the new sneakers that Mom had bought me. Actually, they were pretty cool. Just a little tight in places. And they were still stiff and shiny. Well, I'd have to get used to them. Leaving the house, I jumped on my bike and went to collect my papers.

Having a paper route is a great way to make money and keep an eye on the neighborhood at the same time. And in my neighborhood there's always something going on. I cycled along my route, tossing newspapers onto everyone's front walk as I rode. As usual, a middle-aged man in a rhinestone-studded bathrobe came out to get his immediately.

"Thank you," he called. "Thank you very much." He spoke in a low musical voice.

"You're welcome!" I called, glancing back. He was already on his way into the house for his breakfast of fried-banana sandwiches. Even out here I could smell them cooking.

And that's when I noticed something strange.

Someone was following me, and he was picking up

one of the newspapers I had thrown. He tossed it into some kind of basket, and then started to move on to the next paper.

I couldn't believe it. Somebody was stealing the papers I was delivering!

"Hey!" I yelled. "What do you think you're doing?" I started pedaling furiously toward the thief. I was too far away to make out his face or anything. All I could see was that he was about my size and age, with blond hair and the weirdest backpack I've ever seen. It was all silver and glittery.

And he was riding a bicycle that didn't have any wheels. I don't mean that the wheels had been stolen or anything, but that it didn't seem to *need* them. It just seemed to float in the air, about the same distance off the ground as if it had wheels. The basket behind him was floating in the air, too. And it wasn't attached to him or the bike by anything.

I have to admit that, in all my time in Eerie, I'd never seen anything like this before.

"What do you think you're doing?" I called out again.

The thief looked up and realized he'd been spotted. Immediately he whirled the bike around and sped away at least three times faster than I could go on my bike. The basket followed along behind him in the air, like a dog running after its owner on a walk.

I didn't bother trying to chase the kid. Instead, I checked to see how many papers he'd stolen. It looked like he'd only grabbed four, but he was clearly after more. Luckily, I was near the end of my route at this point, so I finished it and reported the theft of the four papers to my boss. He promised to call Sergeant Knight at the police station and report it. Then he gave me four papers and I redelivered them.

But I was puzzled. Why would anyone want to steal four copies of the same paper? I mean, he could hardly be making a profit selling them. And if he just wanted to read one, he would have taken just one.

And then there was his crazy bike. It obviously had to have some kind of motor in it, but it hadn't made any noise. It might have been some kind of new invention I'd never heard of before, but I seriously doubted it. Wouldn't something like that be all over the news?

So . . . what was it? As usual, I didn't have a clue—yet.

On the bus to school, I told Simon all about it and we agreed that we should look into the situation. Simon's pretty neat, for a younger kid. He's very smart, and he's got lots of guts. We make a great investigative team. His eyes widened as I told him about the thief. "Neat!"

"Yeah." I shook my head. "I wish I'd managed to

get a better look at him. It could have been any blond-haired kid from my grade.''

"Well, at least you scared him off," Simon said.

"Maybe." I wasn't so sure about that. "But this is Eerie, don't forget. You can't scare off weirdness just by yelling at it. At least, it's never worked that way before."

I was sure that I'd be seeing more of the thief pretty soon. Since Simon was two grades below me, we went to our separate classes, agreeing to meet up for lunch.

In homeroom, my teacher, Mr. Dupries, gave the usual announcements, ending with the fact that Mayor Culpa would be speaking at a special assembly for the whole school the following Monday morning, and we should all at least try to look presentable for it. Then he smiled at us, which usually meant bad news.

"And we have a new student with us for a while," he said brightly. He waved his hand toward a new kid sitting at the front of the class. "This is Jazen Karter, class. I hope you'll all be very friendly, and show him what a nice town this is. He's staying here temporarily with his grandfather, Mr. Foreman."

Jazen looked around and smiled shyly at the class. He was blond-haired, and about the build of the thief I'd chased earlier. Was it possible that he was my thief? I didn't smile back. I decided that it might be smart to keep an eye on him.

On the way to our first class I introduced myself. "Marshall Teller," I told him, sticking out my hand. He just stared at it, as if nobody had ever offered to shake hands with him before and it was a custom he'd never even heard of. Well, it takes all kinds, so I let my hand fall. "Welcome to Eerie."

"Thanks, Marshall," he said, blushing slightly. Could it be guilt? I'd find out soon enough. "Seems like a nice town."

"Yeah. It *seems* like one," I agreed. Jazen looked fairly normal, but there was something odd about him I couldn't quite pin down. Then it clicked. He was wearing a Grateful Dead T-shirt. But his was spelled "Great Full Dead." Maybe it was some kind of a joke—I couldn't tell, but it definitely added to his weirdness factor. "So, how long are you stuck here for?" I asked.

"I'm not quite sure," he replied. "It depends."

"On what?"

He shrugged. "Things."

Well, you couldn't argue with *that,* could you?

2 WEIRD
EERIE
INDIANA

The Center of Weirdness for the entire planet

FOX KIDS network
© 1997 Fox Kids

EERIE INDIANA is the center of weirdness for the entire planet, the number one landing site for UFOs in the country... But for some strange reason, only 13-year-old Marshall Teller and his 10-year-old friend Simon Holmes notice it!

Watch the #1 hit television series every week!